To Neil and Lizzy, with love

OPERATION GADGETMAN!

Malorie Blackman

Illustrated by Neil Chapman

First published in 1993 by
Doubleday
This Large Print edition published by
BBC Audiobooks by arrangement with
Random House Children's Books 2005

ISBN 1 4056 6095 3
Text copyright © Oneta Malorie
Blackman, 1993
Illustrations copyright ©
Neil Chapman, 2005

British Library Cataloguing in Publication Data available

Printed and bound in Great Britain by
Antony Rowe Ltd., Chippenham, Wiltshire

Contents

Chapter One

A Little Experiment!

BOOM! WHIIIZZ! KER-BOOOM!
The whole house shook and the windows rattled violently. Gadgetman was at it again! Beans was still for only a moment. She ran out of the bathroom and dashed downstairs, her toothbrush in her hand.

'Dad! Dad, what's going on?' Beans yelled.

A high-pitched whistle shrieked

1

through the house again. Beans ran into the kitchen.

BOOOOM! WHIZZZ!

'Eeek!' Beans threw herself down on to the kitchen floor.

Only just in time, too! A small red-and-yellow doobry-whatsit whizzed through the open kitchen window and shot over her head, before veering left to crash into a box of cornflakes.

BOOOOOOM!

Beans shook her head as she got to her feet. Dad could blow up his workroom if he wanted to—and he often did!—but did he have to blow up the kitchen as well? Dad's workroom was at the bottom of the garden, but there were times when the bottom of the garden wasn't far enough away. Beans didn't mind her dad being an inventor—much!—but did he have to make so much noise about it?

'Beans, are you OK?' Beans's dad called through the kitchen window.

'Yes, Dad.' Beans frowned. 'What on earth are you doing? You didn't tell me your animal crunchies were meant to explode like that!'

2

'They're not! I got the propellent mixture wrong. I'd better stop the rest of them from blowing up as well! Bye!' Beans's dad started across the garden. He stopped abruptly and turned back. 'Beans, er . . . you won't say a word to your friends about what happened on Wednesday night, will you?'

'No, Dad.'

'Our secret?'

'Our secret,' Beans agreed. As if she would tell anyone. No way!

Beans went out into the hall. Another explosion sounded behind her. She raised her eyes heavenwards, then walked faster.

I don't have time for all this. I have to get ready for school, Beans thought firmly.

She started up the stairs, vigorously brushing her teeth, when the doorbell rang. With a sigh, she turned to open the door. She'd never get to school at this rate!

It was her two best friends, Louisa and Ann. They always walked to school together. Beans grinned, the toothpaste frothy and bubbling in

3

her mouth.

'Arrgh! Mad girl! Mad girl! Call the RSPCA!' Ann took a hasty step backwards.

Beans laughed, before choking on the toothpaste.

'Ugh! Beans, do you have to?' Louisa wrinkled up her nose. 'That is so gross!'

WHIZZZZ!

They all jumped.

'What on earth was that?' Ann asked, her green eyes round like saucers. 'Your dad?'

Beans nodded. Who else would be making that kind of racket at eight-fifteen in the morning? Mr McKee, their neighbour, would be knocking on the front door for sure with all that din.

'It sounds like he's trying to give everyone in the street a heart attack.' Louisa frowned.

Beans shrugged, then pointed to her mouth and darted up the stairs. Tooth-paste rinsed out, she ran back downstairs to the hall to join her friends. Dad was there ahead of her. His hair was sticking up in tufts all over

4

his head, his glasses were practically off his nose, and the right-hand arm of his glasses was sticking in his ear rather than resting on top of it. He was wearing a blue T-shirt and the shorts Beans had bought him for Christmas— the ones with Bugs Bunny playing tennis all over them. And he only had one slipper on.

'Is everyone sure they're all right?' Bean's dad asked anxiously.

Louisa nodded. Ann bit her bottom lip and lowered her eyes, trying her best not to laugh. Beans couldn't blame her! Why did Dad have to be *so* embarrassing!

'I was doing a little experiment and it . . . er . . . went ever so slightly wrong,' he said.

'As always!' Beans muttered.

'Pardon, dear?'

'Nothing, Dad,' said Beans, hastily. 'Rats! I've forgotten my jacket. I'll be right back.' And she ran upstairs to her room.

When she came downstairs again, Dad said, 'I'm just telling your friends about my latest invention—animal crunchies! They're biscuits, shaped like various animals, which actually cook as you propel them through the air! Mind you, you have to lob them quite a few times before the ingredients cook properly, but it's worth it, 'cause then you get hot, fresh shortcake biscuits! Isn't that terrific! I got the idea for them by accident, actually. It was . . .'

'Dad, you'll have to hold your horses until this afternoon or we'll be late for school.' Beans glanced down at her watch.

'But it won't take long . . .'

'We don't have the time, Dad— honest,' Beans said.

'Oh . . . OK then,' her dad said sadly.

Beans sighed. 'Louisa and Ann are coming round for dinner tonight so you can explain how your oojee-whatsits work later,' she said. Her dad's forlorn expression had got to her!

'All right then.' He brightened up. 'I'll make sure there's plenty of food ready for all of you when you get here.'

'Thank you, Mr Conran.' Louisa smiled. 'Yeah, thanks, Mr C.,' said Ann.

Beans turned to lead the way out of the house when her dad piped up from behind her, 'Oh, just a minute, everyone.'

He trotted into the kitchen. Beans looked at her watch again, tapping her foot.

'Beans, if I have to stay behind after school to write another essay for being late, my arm will drop off,' Louisa whispered.

'And my mum will go into orbit,' Ann added.

'DAD . . . !'

'Here we are.' Beans's dad came out of the kitchen, a small black plastic briefcase in either hand. 'There you are, Ann. This one's for you,' he said, handing over one case to Louisa. 'And this one is for you, Louisa,' he continued, handing the second briefcase to Ann.

'Dad, you've got them round the wrong way—again,' Beans said patiently. She pointed to Louisa. 'That's Louisa.' She pointed to Ann. 'And that's Ann! I *have* told you before.'

7

'Oh yes, so you have,' her dad said vaguely. 'Sorry.'

Beans tutted. How could he get her friends mixed up? Louisa was black and Ann was white, for goodness sake!

'Thank you very much, Mr Conran. It's very kind of you.' Louisa looked down at the briefcase in her hand. 'Er . . . what is it?'

'They're Gadgetman spy kits!' Beans's dad announced proudly. 'They're going to be in the shops from the end of this month. Tell your friends! Tell your parents! Tell everyone! Buy now before the Christmas stampede.'

It was only June.

'Oh, Dad!' Beans shook her head.

If she shook it any more that morning it would drop off her neck! Some fathers shouldn't be allowed, they really shouldn't.

Especially hers!

P R I N N N N N G ! PRRINNNNNGG! Someone was pressing the doorbell and they obviously *weren't* going to take their finger off it until the front door opened.

8

Beans and her dad looked at each other.

'Mr McKee!' they said in unison.

Beans's dad turned round to scarper back to his workroom.

'Oh no you don't, Dad. Stay where you are!' Beans opened the door.

'Beans, I'd like to speak to your father about all those explosions going off in your garden, please,' Mr McKee said tersely. He looked past Beans and saw who he was looking for. His dark, bushy eyebrows fell so low over his narrowed eyes that they practically touched his kneecaps.

'Dad, we'll see you later,' Beans pulled Louisa and Ann out the front door with her.

'Er . . . Beans, couldn't you . . .' her dad began.

'Sorry! No can do! We'll be late for school if we hang around much longer,' Beans said.

'Mr Conran, I'm fed up! I'm warning you—one more bang, one more explosion, just one more teeny-tiny *pop* and I'm calling the police!' ranted Mr McKee.

9

Beans and her friends didn't wait to hear any more. They left her dad on the front doorstep, discussing his latest invention and the noise it made with his irate neighbour.

The three girls marched quickly down the hill.

'Why didn't you stay behind? Your dad obviously wanted you to,' Louisa said.

'Dad has to learn to get himself out of trouble,' Beans retorted. 'I can't keep doing it for him all the time.'

'Where did he get his animal crunchies idea from?' Ann laughed. 'I've never heard of anything like that before.'

'Is it any wonder!' Beans said dryly. 'Who else would come up with an idea like that?'

Louisa looked down at her watch. 'I hate to tell you two this, but . . .' She didn't need to say the rest.

Without any of them suggesting it, they all started running. They were going to be late for school.

Again.

Chapter Two

Gadgetman Goes Missing!

'Oooh! I'm dying to see what's in it.' Ann fiddled with the clasps on the briefcase. 'I would have opened it in the street, but knowing my luck everything in it would've decorated the pavement two seconds afterwards.'

Assembly had finished, but Mr Lark hadn't yet appeared to take the class for double geography. Louisa already had her briefcase on her desk, about to open it.

'Look, everyone! Look what Beans's dad gave us,' Ann preened. 'Dead-brill spy kits!'

There was a huge crowd around them in seconds. Beans was almost trampled underfoot in the rush.

'Beans calls her dad "Gadgetman". That's his job—he invents things, gadgets,' Louisa explained. 'And he gave us these.'

SNAP! SNAP! SNAP! SNAP!

The clasps on the black plastic briefcases sprung back.

'Oooohhhh!'

'Look at that . . .'

'Wow!'

Even though Beans knew what was in the briefcases, she was still excited. Dad would have loved this reaction! She stood up on a chair to peer over everyone else's heads.

'There's an instruction book here.' Ann picked up the manual on top of everything else in the briefcase and turned a couple of pages. She began to read. "Gadgetman Spy Kit Contents List: Special two-way pencil, torch

12

(batteries not included), mirror, tweezers, magnifying glass, notepad, evidence bags, black-and-white fingerprint powder, fingerprint brush, TOP SECRET folder . . ." '

'Did your dad really make all that?' Stephen turned round to ask Beans.

Beans nodded, her face growing more and more warm. 'Dad had the idea and he wrote the instruction book. That has things in it like secret codes, masks and disguises, following suspects, the proper way to take fingerprints and all kinds of other stuff. Then Dad sent his idea to a toy company and they put the whole lot together.'

'What's a . . . a special two-way pencil?' Jessica asked.

'Half of it is a normal graphite pencil,' Beans explained. 'The other half has got specially treated wax down the middle. When you write with the wax end it doesn't show up until you do special things to it. It's all in the instruction book.'

'And are all the spy kits the same?' asked Stephen.

Beans nodded.

'Can I have one?' Stephen asked eagerly.

'And me . . .'

'Me too . . .'

'I don't know if Dad's got any more,' Beans said quickly.

No way did she want the whole class camping out in her front garden.

'Mr Conran said the kits are going to be on sale at the end of this month,' Louisa called out over the noise of everyone in the class asking Beans for a spy kit.

'WHAT IS GOING ON IN HERE?' Mr Lark's voice boomed out from behind everyone, making them all jump. 'Beatrice Conran! What are you doing standing on that chair? Would you stand on your chairs at home?' he asked.

Beans opened her mouth to say that she often did, but Mr Lark got in first.

'No, of course you wouldn't,' he said, answering his own question. By this time everyone else had darted back to their own desks.

'Louisa, Ann, come to the front of

the class—and bring those cases with you,' Mr Lark ordered.

He pulled his glasses down to the end of his nose, the better to scrutinize everyone. Beans couldn't be sure which glinted more, his piggy eyes or his snooker-ball bald patch, which went from the top of his forehead practically all the way back to his nape. She hated geography!

'It's a spy kit, sir,' Louisa explained.

'Don't be facetious, child!' Mr Lark snapped.

When he saw what was in the cases Mr Lark said, 'Right then! These are confiscated until the end of school. And you two will stay behind in detention for an hour this afternoon and write me an essay, entitled "Why I was unwise to bring my toys to school . . .".'

'Oh, but sir . . .' Ann began.

'No buts.' Mr Lark raised a hand. 'Or you can both stay behind on Monday afternoon as well.'

Ann shut up.

'But sir, it's Friday,' Beans protested on her friends' behalf 'We all had

15

things planned . . .'

'Then you'll just have to *un*plan them, won't you,' Mr Lark retorted. 'And as you're so concerned about your friends, Beatrice Conran, you can stay behind with them this afternoon. Your essay will be entitled "Why I should not stand on school chairs".'

Beans's mouth fell open.

'I thought you'd appreciate that.' Mr Lark's eyes held a satisfied gleam.

'We should have just ambled to school and had done with it,' Beans muttered under her breath. 'We always end up with detention anyway.'

'Did you say something, Beatrice?' Mr Lark's eyes narrowed.

'No, sir, nothing,' Beans replied quickly.

'Are you sure?'

'Positive, sir,' Beans said innocently.

'Good! Because I have plenty of other essay titles in my head, you know.'

I don't doubt it, Beans thought sourly, but wisely she said nothing.

*   *   *

Beans, Louisa and Ann walked up the steep hill that led to Beans's house. It was late afternoon. A few cotton-wool clouds were dotted about the sky. Beans wiped her forehead. She'd have a shower later if she was still this hot and sticky.

She glanced across the street. A bearded man, wearing sunglasses, sat behind the wheel of a navy-blue Ford Escort. There was someone beside him, but that person was bending down, picking up something off the floor. Beans couldn't be sure if the person in the passenger seat was a man or a woman. She wouldn't have noticed the driver at all except that he was drumming his fingers on the steering wheel and looking directly at her. Beans wondered what the man was doing there. She knew the Escort didn't belong to any of the neighbours.

'I wonder who he's waiting for?' Beans said to her friends.

'Who?' Ann asked.

'Him.' Beans turned to point to the Escort. The driver was looking straight ahead now

'Who cares!' Ann said. 'Beans, you're dead nosy!'

Beans smiled. Ann was right!

They reached Beans's house and walked up the path to her front door.

'Beans, I can only stay for an hour at the most,' Louisa said.

'Me too,' said Ann.

Beans sighed and nodded as she opened her front door. It was all Mr Lark's fault! Her friends would only have time for a quick snack. Beans hoped Dad hadn't gone to too much trouble.

'Gadgetman, we're here!' she yelled, the moment she stepped over the doormat.

Her dad liked it when Beans called him Gadgetman. He said it made him feel like a superhero!

There was no answer.

'Gadgetman, where are you?' Beans shouted.

Still no answer.

'He must be in his workroom. Come on, let's go round the side of the house and surprise him,' Beans suggested.

She led the way out of the front

door, through the side gate and down the path. The workroom was really a large shed, as tall as it was broad. Once it had been a magnificent, solid structure. These days, although it was still solidly patched, years of explosions and experiments gone wrong had taken their toll. And now there was a huge hole in the roof where there had been none the day before. From the looks of it, the door had taken quite a bashing too.

So much for her dad's new gadget!

Beans pushed at the door which was hanging half off its hinges. They all stepped into the workroom.

'Oh no! Call the police—you've been burgled!' Louisa exclaimed.

Beans frowned at her, then at Dad's workroom, then back at Louisa. 'It always looks like this,' she said, annoyed.

Louisa mumbled a small 'Oh!'

'Cheek!' Beans grinned. 'It's not that bad!' In fact, if anything, Dad blowing it up that morning had made it neater!

The workroom was still—almost eerie in its stillness, with wires and cables and printed circuit boards and

19

light bulbs and switches and batteries and a host of other electronic gadgetry scattered everywhere.

'That's strange!' Beans mused. It usually takes a crowbar to get Dad out of here. I wonder where he is?'

Back in the house, Beans called for her dad again. There was no answer. They all ambled into the kitchen. Surprisingly, there was no food laid out on the work surface waiting for them. No sandwiches, no plates of biscuits, no bowls of crisps and peanuts. Nothing in the oven. Nothing cooking on the hob. Beans's dad was famous for his yumptious dinners.

Instead of food there was an envelope. The envelope had 'Beatrice' written on it in her dad's squirly-whirly handwriting.

Instantly, Beans knew that something was wrong. Her dad never, *ever* called her Beatrice. It was always Beans. Beans was sure her dad had actually forgotten her real name. She picked up the envelope and frowned down at it.

'What's wrong?' Ann asked, noticing

her friend's expression.

Beans didn't reply. She tore open the envelope, a deep frown turning down the corners of her mouth. Inside was a single sheet of plain white paper. Beans began to read:

dear BEATRICE,

I don't want you to worry or Read anything into this Letter, but Egg-head that I Am, (And a Dolt as well!), I clean forgot to tell you Beatrice that I need some Extra components which I can only get from out of Town. you Mustn't Worry. i'll be home in a day or so, although It might take an Extra bit of time For your soft-boiled Egg-headed father to find the Component he Needs.

THE fridge is well stocked so help yourself—as if I need to Let you know you can! I'll see you In The Near future, possibly On sunday. phone your gran to come and stay with you until i get back.

all my love,
dad.

p.s. we need some Eggs and you might Buy me some Sausages as well.

'Does your dad often go away by himself for days at a time?' Louisa asked, surprised.

Beans shook her head. 'No, never,' she replied, shocked.

'Doesn't your dad write dead funny!' Ann said from over Beans's shoulder. 'There are capital letters in the middle of sentences and he's started sentences with small letters. Miss Brace, our English teacher, would have a fit if she saw that.'

'Dad has never written me a letter like this one before. And he doesn't even like sausages.' Beans frowned. 'And he never calls me Beatrice. There's something going on here.'

'What?' Ann asked, surprised.

'That's just it,' Beans said. 'I don't know. But something's wrong. Something's definitely wrong.'

Chapter Three

Gadgetman's Letter

They all trooped into the sitting-room and sat down, Beans between Louisa and Ann. Then they huddled over the letter. There was something there— Beans just knew it. If only she could put her finger on it. Well . . . there was the way the letter was writ-ten, for a start. Dad's writing was terrible, but even he knew that you started sentences with a capital letter and you didn't just chuck them in whenever you felt like it . . .

'That's it! The capitals!' Beans bounced so hard that she almost bounced herself off the sofa.

'What about them?' Louisa frowned.

'Someone get a pen and paper out quick!' Beans directed.

Ann got out the notepad and pencil from her spy kit.

'I'm going to read out all the capitals Dad's written in this letter, and Ann, you can write them down. OK?' Beans said.

'Gotcha,' Ann nodded.

'What are you doing?' Louisa complained. 'I don't get it.'

'You would if you'd read the instruction book in your spy kit,' Beans told her. 'Dad's trying to tell me something. I just know he is. I reckon the capitals are some kind of code. The first set of capitals spell my name— Beatrice. That's not in code, I'm sure. I think that's just to get my attention by using my full yukky name, so put a comma after that and then begin a new line. Right . . . let me see . . . It begins,

24

I R-L-E-I-A-A-D-I . . .'

Beans glanced over to make sure Ann was writing down all the letters. Louisa moved to sit on the other side of Ann.

'That doesn't spell anything.' Louisa stared down at what Ann was writing.

'Of course it doesn't. Not yet,' Beans said. 'That would be too easy. Where was I?'

She carried on reading out all the other capital letters in her dad's note. It took longer than she thought it would. Beans read them out first and then got Louisa to read them out again as a double-check for Ann.

'Put the letters T-H-E together because Dad did,' Beans said doubtfully. 'Maybe he means for those letters to be left together, like the ones in my name at the top of his note.'

At last they finished.

'So what do we do now?' Ann frowned as she scrutinized what she'd just written.

BEATRICE,
I-R-L-E-I-A-A-D-I-B-I-E-I-T-M-W-

I-E-F-E-C-N
  THE,
  I-L-I-I-T-N-O-E-B-S

'What does that mean?' Louisa asked.

'Haven't a clue.' Beans shrugged. 'It's one of Dad's games, so I guess we go through some of his code suggestions. Louisa, what's the first secret code he talks about in the instruction book? I can't remember.'

Louisa took the book out of her spy-kit briefcase and turned past the introduction to the chapters on secret codes and ciphers.

'Er . . . blah . . . blah . . . Here! This looks promising! "The simplest code is one where every alternate or third high-lighted letter should be crossed out."' Louisa read from the book. '"This type of code is particularly useful for the spy who has to leave a message in a hurry and . . ."'

'Yeah, yeah!' Beans interrupted. 'Never mind the rest yet. Let's try what he says?'

'OK, I'll cross out every other letter

after your name,' Ann said slowly. 'Let's see. Leave the "I", cross out the "R", leave the "L" . . .'

The silence in the sitting-room was deafening as Louisa and Beans watched Ann cross out every other letter after Bean's real name except for in the word 'THE'.

BEATRICE,
I-L-I-A-I-I-I-M-I-F-C
THE,
I-I-T-O-B

'That doesn't make much sense,' Louisa said.

'No, it doesn't,' Beans agreed, just as disappointed.

'Let me write out the whole lot again and this time I'll try crossing out every third letter,' suggested Ann.

'Beans, do you really think it's a coded message?' Louisa asked doubtfully as Ann wrote.

'I think it must be. Why would Dad write it so strangely otherwise?' Beans replied. 'But he's probably just doing it as a joke so we have to use our spy kits.'

Beans tried to tell herself that it was the only logical explanation, but that didn't explain the butterflies in her stomach. If Dad was going away, why didn't he tell her beforehand? And why didn't he phone Gran himself? Dad had only been away from home overnight once before. Then he'd told Beans two weeks in advance, and Gran had come to stay the day *before* Dad went away. No . . . something strange was going on.

'OK, ready,' Ann said. 'I'll try every third letter now.'

'No, hang on,' Beans interrupted. 'What capital letter did you cross out first after "BEATRICE"?'

'The "R". Why?' Ann asked.

'Try crossing out the "I" first. Then do each alternate letter after that.' Beans suggested. 'If that doesn't work then we'll try every third letter. We should do the easiest codes first.'

'OK,' Ann agreed. And she began to cross out every other lettet from the first 'I'.

BEATRICE,

R-E-A-D-B-E-T-W-E-E-N THE, L-I-N-E-S

'Look! Look!' Louisa prodded Beans in the ribs. 'It says, "Beatrice, read between the lines".'

'Wow, you're dead right!' Ann stared. 'Read between the lines . . . What does that mean? Isn't this exciting!'

'Maybe your dad means that there's some other meaning to his note besides what he's written?' Louisa suggested.

'No . . . I don't think it's that,' Beans said slowly.

She held the letter to her nose and sniffed at it. Then she held it up towards the sitting-room window

'Ann, put your nose to that and tell me if you smell anything.' Beans handed over the letter.

Ann sniffed hard at it. 'That's dead weird! It . . . it whiffs of . . . candles.'

'Let me have a smell.' Louisa took the letter and put it to her nose. 'You're right. It does,' she said, surprised.

Beans smiled with relief. 'Dad wrote

me a secret message using one of the two-way pencils in the spy kit. That must be what he meant by "Read between the lines". That's where the secret message is between the lines he wrote with the ordinary part of the pencil.'

So it had to be a joke. It just had to be.

'Quick! What does it say?' Ann asked.

'I'll need some . . . now, what is it? . . . some cocoa powder or gravy browning,' Beans remembered. 'It has to be something dark that will stick to the wax and make it show up. I know! Some black finger-print powder ought to do it.'

'Is all this in the instruction book too?' Louisa asked.

Beans nodded. 'Yeah, but it's been a while since I read it.'

'I'm going to read every word in that book tonight,' Ann said. 'Sounds dead interesting!'

'Ann, can't you use some other word to describe things?' Louisa complained. 'Everything is dead this or dead that. It's dead gruesome!'

Ann grinned. Louisa took the jar of black fingerprint powder out of her spy kit and handed it to Beans.

'Right then,' Beans took a deep breath.

She sprinkled some of the powder along the top edge of Dad's note and very lightly brushed the powder down the page. Instantly, the secret words written between the pencil lines of Dad's first message began to appear as the powder stuck to the wax.

'It's working. What does it say?' Ann asked excitedly.

'Chill out, Ann.' Louisa raised her eyebrows. 'It probably says something like "Your dinner is at the fish-and-chip shop . . ."'

'That's what I'm thinking,' Beans said.

But the uneasy, queasy churning in her stomach was back. Beans brushed the powder back up the page and down again, careful not to smudge the wax. Then she turned in the two edges of the letter to pour the remaining powder back into its jar. Dad had written the secret message in very small writing. Beans started to read.

Beans,

I don't want you to worry but I'm being kidnapped. I'm not joking. This is deadly serious. Two men arrived asking for my induction oscillator. They forced their way in and searched through the whole house and my workroom until they found it. I've refused to tell them how my invention works so they're forcing me to leave with them. They told me to write you this letter so that you wouldn't suspect anything was wrong. I'm pretending to do a lot of rubbing out with the wax end of this pencil, so I can write this. Go to the police immediately. Tell them what happened on Wednesday night. I need your help, Beans. Go straight to the police. And be very, very careful.

I love you.

Dad.

No-one said a word when Beans

finished reading. Beans stared down at the letter, reading it twice and a third time.

'It's a joke—right?' Louisa said.

Beans looked at her friends. She shook her head. 'Dad wouldn't play a joke like that.'

'But it can't be real . . .' Ann said what they were all thinking. 'I mean, who would want to kidnap your dad? No-one goes round kidnapping people like that. And your dad's not rich . . .'

'They didn't do it for money. They did it for . . .' Louisa scanned the letter on Beans's lap. 'For an induction oscillator—whatever that is.'

Silence fell over the room like a thick, dark blanket.

'Nah! Come on!' Ann gave a tremulous laugh. 'It can't be true. That sort of thing only happens on the telly. And certainly not in Cleevesdon. Nothing ever happens in this town.'

'But it *has* happened.' Beans didn't recognize her own voice. She suddenly felt very, very cold. She was actually shivering.

She whispered, 'My dad's been

kidnapped.'

Chapter Four

The Police Arrive

Beans stood up. 'I'm going to the police.'

'We're coming with you,' Louisa said.

'Dead right,' Ann agreed.

'No, you'll both be late home.' Beans wrapped her arms around herself in an effort to stop trembling. 'It's getting late.'

'Beans, are you all right?' Louisa asked anxiously.

Beans clamped her teeth together to stop herself shaking, but it did no good. 'No. Why am I shaking so much?'

'I think you're in shock. My mum's a nurse so I know what I'm talking about.' Ann stood up and wrapped her arms around Beans. 'What you need is a cup of tea or something hot and you need to keep warm.'

'I'll make the tea,' Louisa volunteered. 'I'll just go and . . .'

'No, we don't have time. I must tell

the police,' Beans interrupted.

'If you phone them, they'll think it's just some kid playing feeble games,' Louisa said.

'Then I'll . . . I'll go to see them—right this second.' Beans found it hard to think straight.

No-one spoke as they all walked out into the hall. Beans retrieved her jacket from over the banister and put it on. The door-bell rang.

'I'll get it.' Louisa went to the front door and opened it.

'Beatrice Conran?' A tall man with wavy light brown hair and piercing dark blue eyes moved to stand in the doorway. He wore black cord trousers, a blue shirt and a black leather jacket. He was an oak of a man, solidly built and very muscular, but not fat.

'I'm Louisa, that's Beans I mean Beatrice.' Louisa pointed behind her with a frown. 'Can we help you?'

The man's intense gaze shifted to Ann and Beans. 'Can I come in?' he asked.

'We're not buying anything.' Ann moved to stand beside Louisa, blocking

36

the door. A door-to-door salesman was the last thing any of them needed at the moment. Beans came up and stood before her friends.

'I'm not selling anything,' the man said easily. He took out a wallet from his inside jacket pocket. Opening it, he waved it under Beans's nose before putting it back where he took it from. 'I'm Detective Warner from the CID division of Cleevesdon police station. I've come to speak to your father.'

'You're from the police?' Beans blinked rapidly.

Detective Warner nodded. 'Is your father in?'

'No. No, he isn't,' Beans said quickly. 'We were just coming into town to see you. When I got home, this letter was waiting for me. Dad's been kidnapped.'

Beans took the carefully folded letter out of her jacket pocket where she'd just put it, and handed it over. With a deep frown, Detective Warner took the letter and started to read.

'Dad wrote the secret bit in between the lines of his other message,' Beans explained. 'You see—he's been kidnapped. He says so.'

'This is a joke—right?' Detective Warner said slowly.

'Of course it isn't. Look at Dad's letter. Look!' Beans urged.

Detective Warner did as directed. 'I see . . . May I come in?'

Beans and Ann stepped aside. Detective Warner came into the house.

'The sitting-room's through there.' Beans pointed the way.

Once they were all seated, Beans watched as Detective Warner read Dad's letter over again. 'You say your dad left you this secret message?'

'Yes, he used a two-way pencil,' Ann answered before Beans could. 'Beans made the message appear by using black finger-printing powder. The capital letters in the first message were the clue. They spelt out "Beatrice, read between the lines" in code!'

Detective Warner scrutinized the note. After a few moments he gave a low whistle. 'Very ingenious.'

'But how did you know Dad had been kidnapped?' Beans asked, confused. 'I didn't call you.'

'That's not actually why I called round,' Detective Warner said slowly. 'Yesterday, his building society got in touch with us about a letter they'd received from your father. A letter containing a lot of money and information about one of his inventions. An induction oscillator?'

'A what?' Ann said. 'Oh, the thing he mentioned in his note.'

'It is a bit of a mouthful,' Detective Warner agreed.

'What about it?' Beans asked with a frown. 'Dad gave the building society their money back.'

Ann and Louisa exchanged a puzzled glance.

'What money?' Louisa mouthed.

Ann shrugged.

'Yes, I know he gave it back and he's to be commended for it,' said Detective Warner. Not everyone would have been so honest. The building society got in touch with us at the police station as we have more resources than they do. I came round to see your father to get more details on exactly how the thing works. That way we can alert the

39

other banks and building societies nationwide.'

'Beans, what's this induction oscillator thing, then?' Louisa asked.

'Dad built it to test out the specific circuits and logic functions on printed circuit boards and other stuff,' said Beans impatiently. 'I think Dad said its full name is a programmable, positive feedback, induction inter-oscillator . . . or something like that.'

Louisa raised her eyebrows. 'Of course it is! I should have guessed that for myself!'

'I don't know what that means, but it sounds dead good,' said Ann, impressed.

Beans turned to Detective Warner. 'My dad's been kidnapped. What are we going to do?'

'I think before we go any further you should tell me what happened on Wednesday night, just as your dad instructed in his note to you,' Detective Warner said slowly. 'There might be a clue in there somewhere as to who's got your father.'

Beans looked from Ann and Louisa

40

to the detective, wondering what she should do.

'I'm not sure I should tell you,' Beans said uncertainly. 'I mean, I promised Dad that I wouldn't tell anyone.'

Detective Warner held up her dad's letter. 'But in his note to you he says you should tell us everything. Don't miss anything out, no matter how trivial you think it is. It might be a clue to his kidnappers.'

Put that way, Beans felt she had no choice.

'It's just that that . . . Dad was working on one of his gadgets on Wednesday evening—the induction oscillator,' Beans began reluctantly, still feeling uncomfortable. 'When I got home from school, Dad needed a special kind of wire for his oscillator, so he said we should go to the DIY shop and afterwards we could have a pizza for dinner.'

'I wish my mum would do that more often,' Ann said.

'I wish my mum would do that just once!' sighed Louisa.

'Anyway, Dad drove us to the DIY shop. But just before we went in, I told him to make sure he had his cheque book or his credit cards or some money on him,' Beans continued. 'Whenever we go shopping, Dad always waits until we're supposed to pay before he remembers that he didn't bring any money out with him. I didn't want to go through all that again.'

'And did he have any money?' Detective Warner asked.

Beans shook her head. 'He only had one of those cards that lets you take money out of automatic cash-dispenser machines. You know, the ones outside banks and building societies. So we had to drive into the centre of town to use the machine outside his building society to get some money. That's when it happened.' Beans stopped talking.

'Go on. I'm listening,' Detective Warner said gently.

'Dad didn't do anything wrong, I promise he didn't,' Beans said earnestly. 'It wasn't his fault.'

'What wasn't his fault?' the detective asked.

'Dad . . . Dad put his induction oscillator on the cash dispenser and gave me his card. He always lets me take the money out. He types in his number but I do the rest. I was checking the expiry date on his card whilst D-Dad started fiddling about with the oscillator—typing in commands and numbers and things . . .' Beans trailed off.

'And?' Louisa prompted before the detective could.

'There was this funny click-clicking sound and then . . . and then a whole load of money came spewing out of the machine,' Beans mumbled.

'Money! You're joking!' Ann stared at Beans.

'I wish I was,' Beans said unhappily. 'A whole load of ten- and twenty-pound notes poured out of the machine, even though Dad and I tried to put our hands over the money slot to keep them from coming out. There were so many notes they started falling on the ground. It was so embarrassing. Luckily, there was no-one around at the time or it would have been even

43

worse.' Beans looked at Detective Warner, her eyes wide with anxiety. 'Dad didn't mean any harm—honest he didn't.'

'What commands and numbers did your dad type into this oscillator?' Detective Warner leaned forward.

'I don't know,' said Beans unhappily. 'I wasn't really paying attention until all the money started falling out.'

'So how much was there?' Louisa asked.

'Five thousand and seventy pounds,' Detective Warner answered. 'At least, that's what your dad gave back to the building society . . .'

Ann stared at Beans. 'Five thousand and seventy . . .'

'That's all there was, I swear,' Beans said miserably.

'Wow!' Louisa breathed.

'Dad . . . Dad put all the money in an envelope with a letter explaining what had happened and posted it through the building society's letterbox,' said Beans. 'The building society was shut, otherwise we could have gone in there and then. After that we went straight home. We didn't go to the DIY shop or try Dad's card in the machine or anything. Besides, there wouldn't have been any point. The cash dispenser didn't have any more money in it.' Beans looked at Detective Warner, her eyes wide. Did he believe her? He had to believe her.

'Did you see the letter your dad wrote?' Detective Warner asked at last.

Beans nodded. 'Yeah, it was addressed to the manager of the building society. Dad explained what had happened and said that anyone with enough know-how could make an induction oscillator just like his that would do exactly the same thing. He offered to visit them and show them exactly what he did to get the money out so they could stop it happening in future.'

Beans swallowed hard. How could she make the police understand? It was an *accident*.

'Do you know how your dad's invention works?' asked the detective.

'Dad explained it to me, but I only got some of it.' Beans frowned.

'Apparently, when you put your card into those machines, a computer reads the magnetic strip on the back of your card and gets your card number and the maximum amount of money you can take out at any one-time, and all kinds of other details. It's only when you key in your card number correctly that you can choose how much money you want to take out. Then the computer sends a signal to the electronic motor which feeds out the money. But when Dad started using his induction oscillator, electrical signals from his gadget bypassed the computer completely and just set the electronic motor going. Dad said that that's how induction in physics works, but I didn't really get the physics bit. Anyway, because the electronic motor hadn't been told by the computer how much money to give out, it gave out the whole lot.'

'Seriously brill!' Ann said, impressed.

'Hhmm!' the detective stroked his light brown eyebrows. 'And of course, the induction oscillator will make any cash dispenser in the country do the same thing.'

'Wasn't your dad even a little tempted to keep the money?' Ann asked.

'Of course not,' Beans said furiously. 'It didn't belong to him.'

'So why didn't your dad just hold the money until the next day, then go in and explain?' Louisa asked.

'Dad said that if he held on to the money for even a day, someone might think that he intended to keep it,' Beans explained. 'Besides, he . . . we both just wanted to get rid of it as soon as possible. It was just sitting in our hands, staring at us . . .'

Beans's face began to burn. It sounded silly, but that's just what had happened. Neither she nor her dad had wanted to keep the money for a second longer than necessary.

'And now your dad's been kidnapped,' Detective Warner said quietly. 'Are you sure there was no-one around when all this money came out of the cash dispenser?'

'I didn't see anyone.' Beans shook her head. 'And I was looking. I didn't want anyone to think we were trying to damage the machine.'

'So what does this induction oscillator whatsit look like?' asked Louisa.

Beans glanced at Detective Warner. His lips were a thin slash across his mouth, his expression stern. She took a deep breath. 'It's . . . it's sort of like one of those small notebook computers you can get. It's got a small keyboard and an LCD screen and all the bits Dad tacked on to it.'

'Would your dad keep notes or blueprints on the induction oscillator about the house?' asked the detective.

Beans shook her head, then shrugged anxiously. 'I don't know. He might do.'

Detective Warner looked straight at Beans. 'We need to get hold of any information on the oscillator before your dad's kidnappers do.'

Beans's heart threatened to burst out of her chest. 'Do you do you think the kidnappers might come back?'

'I don't know. They have your dad so I wouldn't have thought so,' replied the detective. 'But we need to stay one step ahead of them. You must be very careful who you talk to.'

Beans and Detective Warner looked at each other.

'So what are you going to do?' Beans asked desperately. 'You must do something.'

'Don't worry. We intend to,' Detective Warner replied. 'First, do you mind if we keep this letter of your dad's? It will help us with our enquiries.'

Beans shrugged. The sitting-room was still, with everyone deep in thought. From a tree in the back garden, Beans could hear a bird chirping. It sounded so strange, so unwelcome.

'So you believe me?' Beans asked to break the unbearable silence.

Detective Warner nodded. 'Oh yes! We shall certainly start investigating. Tell me, is your mum at home?'

Beans shook her head. 'My mum died over five years ago.'

'Do you have an older brother or sister to look after you?' the detective asked. 'Do they know anything about the induction oscillator?'

'No, I'm an only child. Don't worry, I'll phone my gran. She'll look after me until Dad can come home.'

Detective Warner stood up. 'The next thing to do is to take you down to the station and get a formal statement.'

'We're coming too, aren't we, Louisa.' Ann stood up also.

'Too right.' Louisa got to her feet, followed by a weary Beans.

Detective Warner studied each of the three girls. He frowned. 'On second thoughts, I'd better get the search for your father underway. I'll take all your statements another time. Look, Beans, let me give you my telephone number. It's for my mobile phone, so you can reach me at any time. We're not really supposed to do this, but I want you to feel you can count on me. If you find any blueprints or notes about your dad's invention, please phone me, any time of the day or night. Don't forget!'

'I won't,' Beans replied.

Detective Warner stood up. 'Right then. Got a pen? I'm Detective Julian

Warner and my phone number is four-four-two-nine-five . . .'

Beans wrote quickly on the back of her hand with a felt-tipped pen she got out of her skirt pocket.

'I'll leave now and get back to the police station. We'll start our enquiries straightaway,' said Detective Warner.

They all went to the front door.

'Don't worry, Beatrice. We'll find your father. I'm sure he's safe and sound.' Detective Warner smiled. 'Oh yes, something else . . . I think it would be best if all three of you didn't say a word about this to anyone else. We don't want to put your dad's life in danger, do we?'

'No!' Beans replied emphatically.

'We won't say a word,' Louisa said.

'Not one word,' Ann agreed.

Beans said goodbye to the detective before closing the front door slowly behind him. She scowled at the door, her eyebrows practically knitting together.

'What's the matter, Beans?' Ann asked. 'I know that look.'

'I don't think much of him,' Beans

said with disgust.

'Who? Detective Warner?' Louisa asked, surprised.

Beans nodded. 'He didn't talk about taking fingerprints or trying to find any clues left by the kidnappers or anything.'

'Maybe he's coming back to do that with some of his colleagues?' Louisa suggested.

'Then why didn't he say so?' Beans argued. 'He didn't seem to be very with it. In fact, you two asked me more questions than he did. *I* could do better than that!'

'Well, you've got to let the police do their jobs,' Ann pointed out. 'I'm sure that detective knows what he's doing.'

But Beans wasn't listening. Her eyes held a strange gleam as she stared into space.

'Yeah . . . I *could* do better than that.' Beans's whisper was more to herself than to anyone else. 'Ann, Louisa, *I'm* going to find Dad! Nothing's going to stop me from finding out who the kidnappers are— and where they're holding him.'

Chapter Five

Looking for Clues

Louisa and Ann stared at Beans.

'You're not serious, are you?' Louisa asked. The look on Beans's face answered her question. 'Beans, you can't do that. It might be dangerous.'

'I can't just sit around here doing nothing,' Beans replied. 'And if that detective's in charge of the case, then it seems to me the police need all the help they can get.'

'But what can you do?' Louisa asked.

'Dad wrote in his note that there were two men in the house today who made him write that letter to me,' Beans said. 'So they must have left some clues behind. Footprints, fingerprints something. And I'm going to look for those clues until I find them.'

Louisa frowned at Ann, then back at Beans. 'Then we're going to help you, aren't we, Ann?' said Louisa firmly.

'You can't. You're both expected at home,' Beans pointed out.

'We can easily phone our parents,' Ann said. 'Come on, Beans, you must let us help you. That's what friends are for, after all.'

'But I don't want to get you two into trouble,' Beans said.

'Don't worry. We'll handle our parents,' Louisa said confidently. 'We're not going to leave you to do everything by yourself.'

'Anyway, what about your gran?' asked Ann. 'You told Detective Warner that you were going to phone her.'

'I will do,' Beans said. 'But not now.

I'll phone her a bit later. I don't want Gran disturbing any likely clues. I'll be out in Dad's workroom when you two have finished your phone calls. I want to examine the workroom first, before it gets any darker outside.'

Beans lowered her head. A moment's unwelcome doubt settled over her. Would anything she could do help? Would it really?

'Beans, don't worry. Your dad's all right. I just know he is,' Louisa said gently.

'Yeah! I know it too.' Ann nodded unhappily as she struggled to find something meaningful to say.

Beans smiled at her friends before turning quickly away. Her eyes were in danger of leaking. Louisa and Ann looked at each other. Ann put an arm around Beans's shoulder. Louisa held Beans's hand.

'I . . . I'm glad you two are here with me,' Beans said softly. 'I don't know what I'd do if I had to go through all this alone.'

'Don't even think about that,' Louisa said firmly. 'We're here and we're not going anywhere. Not yet, at any rate!'

Beans smiled gratefully.

She ran upstairs to get the Gadgetman spy kit her dad had given her over a month before. It was behind her dressing-table, just below her bedroom window. Beans bent down to get it and slowly straightened up again, her fingers clenched tightly around the briefcase handle.

Her dad had given her this spy kit.

One of the first to be produced it was. Beans remembered the grin on Dad's face as he handed it to her. Beans had been happy for her dad because he was so pleased about it, but she remembered thinking, now where on earth am I going to put this thing?

At the time she'd seen it as another of her dad's gadgets, cluttering up her bedroom. Beans lifted the case and placed it against her cheek . . .

Where was Dad now? Was he still in Cleevesdon or had he been taken out of town? He might be in Scotland or down in London. He might even be out of the country by now. Beans closed her eyes. If she carried on worrying like

56

this she would go crazy.

Her dad had been kidnapped.

Beans had never felt so useless or helpless. Her eyes began to water again. She stared hard out of her bedroom window, eyelids wide apart to stop herself from blinking the tears down her cheeks.

Come on, Beans. Go downstairs and *do something*, she told herself sternly.

Anything would be better than standing in her room, thinking too much. Beans took a deep breath, then another, waiting for the huge, choking lump in her throat to shrink. She ran downstairs, past her friends in the hall, through the kitchen and out into the garden, eager to get started.

She stood outside the workroom, staring at it. It was hard to know where to begin. How would she be able to tell what was a clue and what wasn't? Beans examined the grass leading up to the workroom. It was short and very dry. No footprints, no tracks of any kind.

'No help there then,' she muttered.

She walked gingerly up to the workroom door, stepping lightly, still scanning the grass for possible clues. Only when she stood directly in front of the workroom did she look up. At once she noticed something. Something that should have struck her before.

She remembered that the last time Dad had blown the door half off its hinges, he had hammered a nail into the outer door-frame. Until he'd fixed the door properly, Dad had used a strong piece of string to tie the door handle to the nail, to stop the door from swinging open and the rain getting at his gadgets. He hadn't done that now. The door was half off its hinges, but he hadn't secured it.

More proof that he had been kidnapped—as if Beans needed any. If Dad had just gone away to buy components, he would have made sure the door was firmly closed. Beans wished she had noticed it earlier so that she could have pointed it out to Detective Warner. This was more proof that it was no joke.

But thinking about it, Beans was sure

that the detective had believed her. He just didn't seem very dynamic. Not her idea of a proper detective at all.

Something caught Beans's eye. There was something on the nail.

She put her spy kit down on the grass and got out the magnifying glass. She moved in for a closer examination of the nail. A long, thin piece of blue plaid material was attached to it. Beans's heartbeat deafened her.

A clue!

It had to be! Using her spy-kit tweezers, Beans plucked the tiny piece of material off the nail and dropped it into an evidence bag. The small, clear plastic bags were perfect for storing any clues she might find. To her surprise—and pleasure—the spy kit was actually *useful*.

'Don't worry, Dad. I'll find you,' Beans muttered.

Now that she was doing something constructive, Beans felt a lot better. She even felt kinder towards that detective. Maybe she had been a little bit unfair on Detective Warner. Like most grown-ups, he wouldn't want to share his thoughts as to what he was doing with a kid, even if it was the kid's dad who had been kidnapped. But Beans couldn't sit around doing nothing.

I'm not that sort, she thought.

Using her magnifying glass, Beans examined the door very closely but could find no further clues. She wondered if she should dust the door handle for finger-prints, but then she wouldn't be able to tell which fingerprints belonged to her dad and which ones belonged to the kidnappers, as she didn't have a record of her dad's.

Beans was still trying to make up her mind what to do, when Ann and Louisa came out into the garden.

'What did your parents say?' Beans said to both of them.

'I have to be back home by eight at the very latest,' Louisa sighed. 'They're so tedious!'

'I told Mum that you'd invited me to spend the weekend with you and that your dad didn't mind, but she reckoned I'd be too much trouble at such short notice,' Ann said with disgust. 'When she began to make noises about speaking to your dad to see if it was really all right, I decided not to push it.'

'Worth a try though,' Beans smiled.

'Worth a try,' agreed Ann.

'So how's it going?' Louisa asked.

Beans held up her first evidence bag. 'This is material I found on the nail over there. One of the kidnappers must have been wearing a blue plaid shirt.'

'Are you sure that wasn't on the nail before today?' Louisa asked.

'I can't be positive, but then where did it come from if it *was* here before today? Dad doesn't have any shirts like that, and I certainly don't,' Beans replied.

'What are you going to do with any evidence you find?' Ann asked.

Beans shrugged. 'I'm not sure. I haven't thought about that bit yet. I guess I'll just hand it over to Detective Warner—when I have some evidence worth something, some evidence he can use.'

'Why don't you store all your information and clues in the TOP

SECRET folder in your spy kit?' Ann suggested.

'That's a good idea.' Louisa raised her eyebrows.

'You needn't sound so surprised.' Ann frowned.

'I'll do that,' Beans butted in before her friends could launch into a full-scale argument. 'We should really call the folder something, though. Some name only we three will know.'

The garden was quiet as they all pondered.

'How about "Project Beans's dad"!' suggested Ann.

Both Beans and Louisa wrinkled up their noses.

'It doesn't exactly flow off the tongue,' Louisa said. 'How about "Project . . ." No, on second thoughts that's a stupid idea.'

Louisa looked hastily at Beans. Talk about insensitive! She'd been about to suggest 'Project Kidnap'. What on earth was wrong with her? This wasn't a game—not at all. It wasn't a film or a joke. Beans's dad really *had* been kidnapped.

'I think I've got a title,' Beans said slowly. 'What do you think of "Operation Gadgetman"?'

Louisa nodded. 'I like it.'

Brill!' Ann grinned.

'Operation Gadgetman it is then,' Beans said.

She squatted down and opened up her TOP SECRET folder. She dropped her first evidence bag into the folder before closing it.

'Next, I thought I'd dust for fingerprints,' Beans said. 'It probably won't do much good, but I have to make sure I've done everything I can.'

'How can we help?' Ann asked.

'I'll need some Sellotape,' Beans said.

'I've got some in my satchel. I'll just go and get it.' Louisa ran back into the house.

'Be careful not to touch anything. I don't want any of the kidnappers' finger-prints smudged or any clues in the house ruined,' Beans called after her. She turned to Ann. 'That goes for you too, Ann. Be very careful what you touch. OK?'

'Gotcha.' Ann nodded.

Gloves! That's what Dad needed in his spy kit. Some thin plastic gloves or maybe they should be cotton? Beans made a mental note to tell her dad when she saw him again. *If* she saw him again . . .' No! Beans shook her head fiercely. *When*—not if.

While Louisa was gone, Beans busied herself with sprinkling black fingerprint powder all over the silver-coloured metal door handle as Ann watched. Then Beans used the fingerprint brush to delicately brush away the excess powder.

'Does it explain how to do all that in your dad's instruction book in the spy kit?' Ann asked, her eyes wide.

Beans nodded. 'Black fingerprint powder for light surfaces and white fingerprint powder for dark surfaces.'

'Wow! You must be so proud of your dad. He's not like most grown-ups, is he? He's not boring at all . . .' Beans straightened up, her lips set.

'Oh Beans, I'm so sorry. I didn't mean to . . . Me and my ginormous mouth,' Ann said, stricken.

64

'It's all right, Ann,' Beans said. 'You're right. My dad may be a lot of things, but he certainly isn't boring. It's just my fault that I didn't appreciate that until now. And I miss him already.'

'Beans, he's all right. I just know he is,' Ann said unhappily.

Beans wiped her hand over her eyes. 'I just wish I could be sure.'

Chapter Six

Gran Arrives

'I've got the Sellotape.' Louisa emerged from the kitchen, a roll of Sellotape in her hand.

Ann gave a secret sigh of relief. She was no good at this kind of thing. She never knew what to say or do when things went wrong with other people and she always just ended up embarrassing everyone. Beans smiled at her.

'It's all right, Ann,' Beans said softly. Ann smiled back.

'Wait a sec, Beans. What about your dad's notes on his oscillator?' Louisa frowned. 'Aren't you going to look for them?'

'Not yet. No way. Finding the kidnappers is the most important thing now, not searching for useless information about Dad's gadget. I don't see how that will help to find him.'

'But Detective Warner said . . .'

'I don't care,' Beans interrupted fiercely. 'It's my dad who's been kidnapped, not his. Looking for stupid notes on the lousy oscillator will just have to wait. And what's more . . . .'

'So what do we do now?' Ann asked, deliberately interrupting.

Beans took a deep breath, then another. She had to calm down. Getting angry wouldn't help anything.

'First, we need a blank sheet of plain paper,' Beans said quietly. 'Then I put two pieces of Sellotape on the front and the back of the door handle and peel them off very carefully. Then I put

67

them on the plain paper. With the dark fingerprint powder I should get a set of prints. That's the theory, anyway.'

'So you've not actually done this before?' Louisa asked.

'Never. And the prints might not even be clear.They might be smudged, or I could smudge them, or I might have two or three sets of prints one on top of the other. Lots of things could go wrong.'

'That's right, Beans, look on the bright side!' Ann teased. 'Or the whole thing might just work first time.'

'Too right. You tell her, Ann,' Louisa joined in.

Beans smiled. They were right. She shouldn't be so pessimistic. She wasn't usually. Moving very slowly and carefully, Beans laid the Sellotape on the outside of the door handle. Once she peeled it off, she held it by its extreme tips before placing it on the plain paper Ann had got out of the kit for her. Next, she did the inside of the door handle. Once that piece of Sellotape had joined the first piece on the paper, they all huddled around for a look. The Sellotape was marked with the dark fingerprint powder and some kind of prints were definitely there.

'The first set of prints are a bit smudged.' Louisa frowned.

'I don't think so,' Beans said. 'I think that's part of a palm print. The second bit of Sellotape has the fingerprints on it. That makes sense. Think about how you'd turn a door handle. Your fingers would be on the *inside* of the handle.'

'But do they belong to your dad or his kidnappers?' Ann asked.

'That's just it,' Beans sighed. 'I have no way of knowing. I'm going to have to try and find some prints that must be Dad's. Meanwhile, these ones can go in the TOP SECRET file along with the other clues. I think . . . Oh no . . !' Beans's face fell.

'What's the matter?' Louisa asked quickly.

'*We* came in here too,' Beans said, stricken. 'Did either of you touch the door handle?'

Ann and Louisa looked at each other.

Ann shook her head. 'I can't

69

remember.' Louisa shrugged helplessly.

'I don't think you did, 'cause the door was already open, wasn't it?' Beans tried to remember.

'I think you should take both our fingerprints as well just to be on the safe side,' Louisa said.

Ann nodded in agreement.

'I'd better do my own as well,' Beans realized.

She took a felt-tipped pen out of her case and coloured in the fingertips of first Louisa, then Ann, then herself. She pressed each of her friends' fingers to a clean sheet of paper, one hand above the other, before doing her own. Beans labelled each sheet of paper very carefully. Ann wiped her fingers on her skirt. Louisa held her hands out in front of her and eyed them with distaste. She stretched out her fingers so that no finger touched the one next to it.

'Yuk! So what next?' Louisa asked.

'Next we go through Dad's workshop with a fine-toothed comb,' Beans said. 'If you find anything, anything at all, let me know.'

Ten minutes and several questions later, they were all getting discouraged. Ann and Louisa thought they found several strange items but Beans had an explanation for each of them.

'This is getting us nowhere,' Beans said reluctantly. 'If there are any other clues in here, then I can't see them. Louisa, you didn't find anything in the corners of the room?'

Louisa shook her head.

'Ann, there was nothing on the windowsill or under it?' Beans carried on.

Ann shook her head. 'Sorry.'

'And there was nothing in the waste-bin?' Beans asked.

Ann and Louisa frowned at each other before turning back to Beans.

'I didn't check in the bin,' Louisa said, surprised. 'I thought you were going to do it.'

'I thought Ann did it,' Beans replied. 'Still, I don't expect we'll find anything in there either.'

'Beans!' Louisa warned.

Beans headed for the bin, mentally telling herself off. If that was the way she really thought, then why bother doing anything at all? She began to fish through the bin.

'Two dead batteries—at least, I'm assuming they're dead . . . bits of wire . . . more bits of wire . . . hang on . . .'

'You've found something?' Louisa asked eagerly.

'So that's where the fish-knife got to!' Beans smiled, regarding the burnt, blackened top of the knife. 'I do wish Dad wouldn't use our cutlery for . . .'

Beans stopped herself in mid-sentence. Dad could burn every knife, fork and spoon in their cutlery drawer as long as he came home safe and well. She carried on searching through the bin.

'Yet more bits of wire . . . an insulating tube . . . Wait a minute . . .'

'What is it?' Ann asked hopefully.

'There's . . .' At this point, Beans stuck her head right in the bin. Ann and Louisa stared at her as if she'd lost her mind.

'Yes, I'm right—there's cigarette ash in here.'

'And your dad doesn't smoke,'

Louisa said, a slow smile spreading right across her face.

'*Exactly.*' Even in the rapidly darkening workroom, Beans's eyes were gleaming. 'And Dad empties this bin every night so the ash had to have been put in there today.'

'What kind of ash is it?' Ann asked.

Beans frowned at her. 'Ann, I'm not Sherlock Holmes, you know! I can't tell the difference between one brand of cigarette ash and another simply by sniffing it.'

'No, I meant is it from a cigar or a pipe or a cigarette?' Ann said.

Silence.

'Good point.' Beans stuck her head into the bin again. 'I'd say it's cigarette ash, but they all smell disgusting to me.'

'Let me have a whiff.' Ann barged Beans out of the way. 'My granddad smokes a pipe so I know that smell.' Ann took a deep breath, her nose over the bin. 'It's not a pipe. It's a cigarette.'

'I suppose it'd be too much to hope for that the cigarette tip is in there?' Louisa said.

Ann shifted through the quarter-full bin. 'No. Just ash,' she said at last.

'I'll put some in an evidence bag, anyway,' Beans said.

Once they were sure that there was nothing else in the workroom, Beans led the way back inside the house.

'You two can check upstairs. Watch where you're both stepping and *don't touch anything.*' Beans warned. Louisa and Ann went to explore the upstairs, whilst Beans phoned her gran.

It only took a few second's deliberation for Beans to decide that she'd wait for Gran to arrive before telling her what had happened to Dad. She couldn't exactly say, 'How are you, Gran? By the way, Dad's been kidnapped!' over, the phone. No, she'd wait until Gran came round and they were alone.

'Gran, it's Beans,' she said, the moment her gran picked up the phone and said hello.

'Well, hello Beatrice, how are you?' Gran asked. Her voice was warm and normal and made Beans sad.

'Er . . . that's what I'm phoning

74

about. Dad isn't here. Can you come over to stay with me until he gets back? He left a note to say I should ask you.' Beans chewed on her bottom lip.

That was about right!

'Where is he?' Gran asked.

'I don't know,' Beans replied. That was truthful.

'Well, when will he be back?'

Beans could hear the frown in Gran's voice.

'I don't know that either. I'll explain when you get here,' Beans said.

'Hmm! I'll be there as soon as possible. In about an hour,' Gran said.

'Thanks, Gran. See you later,' Beans replied.

'Just what is your father playing at?' she heard Gran mutter.

Beans waited for a few seconds before she put down the phone at her end. She was sure she'd done the right thing. It wasn't the sort of conversation to have over the phone.With a sigh, Beans went to join Louisa and Ann.

Forty minutes later the upstairs was done—and not one more clue.

'Downstairs now,' Beans said. 'We'll

have to make this fast. Gran will be here soon.'

It was certainly very tiring work. Beans felt as if she had to examine practically every square centimetre of carpet just so she wouldn't miss anything important. And in spite of careful and detailed scrutiny, there was nothing out of the ordinary in any of the downstairs rooms either.

'Look, Beans, I've got to go home,' Louisa said, glancing down at her watch.

'Oh, no! Is that the time? My mum's going to kill me,' Ann joined in. 'Beans, I'm gonna have to shift.'

'That's OK. Thanks for all your help. It would have taken me for ever to try and do all this by myself,' Beans said gratefully. 'Will I see you both on Monday morning?'

'What are you talking about?' Louisa frowned. 'We're going to be round here first thing tomorrow morning . . . at least I am.'

'I'll be here too, don't worry,' Ann said indignantly.

Beans looked at her friends. She

tried to smile. 'Thanks.' She didn't know what else to say.

'And don't worry, we won't say a word to anyone,' Louisa said. 'Will we, Ann?'

'Dead right! Not one word,' Ann agreed. Just then, the doorbell rang.

'That'll be my gran,' Beans said. She opened the front door, Louisa and Ann behind her.

'Hello, Beatrice. Hello, girls.' Gran stepped over the threshold, closing the door firmly behind her. 'My goodness, but it's getting chilly out there.'

'Hello, Mrs Conran,' Ann said. 'We were just leaving.'

'Don't let me chase you out.' Gran raised her eyebrows.

'You're not—honest. We really were just going,' Louisa said. 'We'll see you tomorrow, Beans,' she added with a whisper. 'Good luck with the fingerprints.'

Beans opened the front door for her friends and watched them as they walked down the hill to the bus stop.

'What fingerprints was Louisa talking about?' Gran asked.

'You heard that!' Beans stared.

'Of course! You young people! You think that once a person passes forty, they're ready to be tucked up in their grave.' Gran grinned 'So what's this about fingerprints?'

'Gran . . . I've got something to tell you,' Beans said unhappily. 'I think you'd better sit down.'

This was it. And it was the worst thing Beans had ever had to do.

At first, Gran wouldn't believe it. A joke in very poor taste, she called it. It was only when Beans convinced her gran to phone Detective Warner that Gran's expression changed from being seriously annoyed with Beans to being seriously worried. Beans listened as Gran spoke to the detective, incredulity and fear growing in her voice. When at last Gran got off the phone, no-one spoke.

'Why didn't you call me, Beatrice?' Gran said at last. 'You should have told me at once. Why didn't you tell me over the phone?'

'I couldn't. I thought it would be better if you were here. If we were together,' Beans sniffed.

Gran beckoned Beans towards her. 'Come here.'

And in the middle of the sitting-room, they silently hugged.

'I think I'll make you a nice cheese omelette,' Gran said firmly, after a few moments. 'You must eat to keep up your strength.'

'Gran!' Beans exclaimed. 'How can you think about cooking at a time like this?'

'Nonsense. You're a growing girl You must give your body something to grow with,' Gran said, already heading for the kitchen.

'But Gran, I couldn't force a thing down,' Beans called after her.

'Nonsense, Beatrice. You'll eat,' Gran called back.

Beans didn't know whether it was a threat or a warning or a promise. She did know, however, that it was useless to argue with Gran once she'd made up her mind on something. Beans silently followed Gran into the kitchen, resentment on her face. What was wrong with Gran? Didn't she *care*?

79

'Beatrice, you have no eggs,' Gran called out, her head buried in the fridge. She straightened up. 'And where are the fresh vegetables and fruit?'

'There's not much in the fridge, Gran, because Dad and I were due to go shopping tomorrow,' Beans explained through gritted teeth.

Gran was not impressed. 'Your father should make sure the fridge is always well stocked. I do. Hhmm! At least there's milk and cheese. I'll make a lovely macaroni cheese.'

Beans shuddered. Macaroni cheese was about as appetizing as a plate of slithery, slimy worms. She scowled at her gran. Dad was missing and all Gran had on her mind was macaroni cheese.

'But before we cook anything, we're going to have to tidy this kitchen,' said Gran. 'You know I can't cook in an untidy kitchen.'

Beans didn't say anything, but she didn't stop scowling. She would never have believed that her gran could be so unfeeling. And she'd never forgive her for it. Never.

'I've got to do . . . do my homework

first,' Beans said icily. 'I'll help you when it's finished.'

She turned round and marched out of the kitchen. Gran didn't care about anyone but herself. Here Beans was, worried sick about Dad and not knowing whether to cry or smash things up or laugh with disbelief or maybe all of them, and what was Gran doing? Making macaroni cheese!

Beans was halfway up the stairs when she paused abruptly. Was she unfair . . .? Hadn't Gran hugged her in the sitting-room? And Beans remembered the look on Gran's face when she was talking to Detective Warner.

Slowly, Beans walked downstairs and back to the kitchen. Gran was bent over, taking a saucepan out of the cupboard. All at once she straightened up, her back still towards her granddaughter. She sniffed and her hands moved to her face. Beans swallowed hard. Unhappily, she realized that Gran was just as upset and worried as she was, only Gran handled it differently. Why hadn't

Beans worked that out for herself?

'Don't worry, Gran. Dad will be all right,' Beans said softly.

Gran spun around. 'Beatrice, child! You frightened the life out of me. Now scat! I don't need you under my feet.'

Beans understood. She smiled faintly. 'No, Gran. My homework can wait. What d'you want me to do?'

Twenty minutes later, Beans was sent out to dump the rubbish in the dustbin in the front garden.

After dinner I'll try and get some of Dad's fingerprints, she thought.

Dad's bedroom would be the best bet. Beans walked out into the front garden and headed for the dustbin which was just by the front gate. She took off the dustbin lid and had almost dumped her bag of rubbish into it when she jumped back, nearly losing her grip on the bag in her hand. There was something on top of the other sealed bags of rubbish in the bin. Something that hadn't been there before. Something that could be important.

An empty cigarette packet.

Chapter Seven

Gran, I'm Frightened

'Gran, can I go and do my homework now, please?' Beans asked.

'My! Such enthusiasm!' Gran pursed her lips. 'So you've finished pushing your macaroni cheese around your plate then?'

Beans nodded.

'Scoot then!' Gran waved her hand. 'I'll clear up by myself.'

Gran had barely finished her

sentence before Beans was out of the sitting-room and halfway up the stairs.

'Thank you, Gran! You're welcome, Beatrice!' Gran said to herself.

'Gran, I heard that!' Beans called out, not stopping.

Beans ran into her bedroom, closing the door quietly behind her. Lying flat on the carpet, she retrieved her spy-kit briefcase from under the bed. She'd put it there after Louisa and Ann had left, not wanting her gran to see what she was up to. Beans sat on her bed, her spy kit in front of her, before opening the case. On top of everything else was the folder, Above the words TOP SECRET, Beans wrote: 'OPERATION GADGETMAN'. Then she opened the folder. What did she have? Ann and Louisa's fingerprints, a partial palm print (anonymous, probably useless), some other fingerprints (anonymous), a piece of material (also probably useless), some cigarette ash and now a cigarette packet—the last three items in evidence bags. Not much to go on. Still, it was a start. Beans held up the evidence bag which contained the cigarette packet, and frowned at it. This packet might have been dropped in their dustbin by any passing stranger. How could she tell? Still, until she checked it out thoroughly, it was a potential clue. So where did all these so-called clues get her?

Answer—nowhere. *Yet.*

With a sigh, Beans sprinkled light fingerprint powder on the black cigarette packet, then carefully brushed off the excess. She examined the box with her magnifying glass. There were fingerprints there all right, but they were so smudged and creased that it was hard to tell where one fingerprint ended and the next one began.

'I'll still keep the packet,' Beans said to herself after a moment's thought.

After all, there might be some other clues on it that she had missed. It might even . . .

'Wait a second . . .' Beans stared down at the box.

She'd just had an idea—an ace idea! She'd dusted the outside of the box, but what about the *inside*?

Using her tweezers, Beans opened the top of the cigarette packet. She tried to think about how she'd hold the packet if she was trying to get out a cigarette. The only likely places for fingerprints were the top or the sides of the inside of it. As the inside of the box was lined with white, tissuey paper, Beans dusted around with the dark finger-print powder. Carefully brushing off the extra again, this time she examined the inside. Her heart began to sledgehammer. There it was a single fingerprint on the inside top of the packet.

'A thumbprint?' Beans wondered.

She searched through her bedside table for some Sellotape. Removing the print would be extremely tricky, and she'd only get one chance to do it right. If she made a mistake, she'd smudge it for sure and then it would be lost for ever. Beans wiped her forehead and pulled her blouse away from her sticky back. She took a deep breath and held it, before placing the Sellotape over the print. It felt like she was shaking all over, as if even her blood was trembling,—but her hands moved slowly and steadily. The moment the Sellotape was over the fingerprint, Beans peeled it straight off again before it had a chance to really stick to the paper. She placed the thumbprint under the other prints she had got that day. Only then did she exhale, breathing deeply to catch her breath. She had done it!

In her best handwriting she added details to each of her labels for each set of prints:

ANN'S PRINTS
    LEFT HAND: THUMB INDEX
    MIDDLE RING LITTLE
    RIGHT HAND: THUMB INDEX
    MIDDLE RING LITTLE

LOUISA'S PRINTS
    LEFT HAND: THUMB INDEX
    MIDDLE RING LITTLE
    RIGHT HAND: THUMB INDEX
    MIDDLE RING LITTLE

MY PRINTS
  LEFT HAND: THUMB INDEX
  MIDDLE RING LITTLE
  RIGHT HAND: THUMB INDEX
  MIDDLE RING LITTLE

PALM PRINT (ANONYMOUS)
  FOUND ON OUTSIDE OF
  DOOR HANDLE TO DAD'S
  WORKROOM

FINGERPRINTS (PARTIAL:
  ANONYMOUS)
  FOUND ON INSIDE OF
  DOOR HANDLE TO DAD'S
  WORKROOM

FINGERPRINT (THUMB?
  ANONYMOUS)
  FOUND ON INSIDE OF
  CIGARETTE PACKET IN
  OUTSIDE DUSTBIN

The next job was to try and find something which would have a good set of Dad's fingerprints on it. Beans went out on to the landing and leaned out over the banister. Gran was downstairs, clattering about in the kitchen. Beans tiptoed into her dad's bedroom and closed the door before switching on the light. Fear, deep and icy cold, bit into her. She was trembling. Here she was in her dad's bedroom—*but where was he?* Beans had never felt so worried. It was a horrible feeling. It ate away at her until she wanted to scream, to let it out.

She took a deep breath and looked around slowly. The state of Dad's bedroom was almost as bad as his workroom. Beans couldn't help but smile. Gingerly, she stepped over coiled wires and plugs and cables and PC keyboards and screwdrivers, scattered all over the carpet. They were all likely places from which to get fingerprints, but there had to be something that would have a good set of fingerprints which wouldn't be smudged from constant handling. And what about Dad's kidnappers? They must have searched in here for the oscillator. Dad said in his letter that they searched all over the house. So how could Beans be sure to get something with her *dad's* fingerprints on it? Beans licked her lips as she looked around the room again. There had to be something . . .'

The light switch on the wall? No, those prints would be smudged for sure. One of Dad's books? No . . . those prints would probably be smudged too.

There must be something . . .

Then Beans saw it.

The light bulb in the bedside lamp! Of course! Dad would only need to put the bulb in once and he wouldn't touch it again until it needed changing. And it was the bayonet kind, not the screw-in kind, so any prints were a lot less likely to be smudged. The only trouble was, how could Beans take it out of its socket without getting her fingerprints all over it? She could wear gloves, but wouldn't that just smudge any prints there might be?

Beans walked over to the bedside lamp. If she was careful, it should be all right. She'd just have to risk it. Using only her palm, Bean pushed the bulb down and twisted it, making sure she was only in contact with the bottom of the bulb and not the sides. It sprang out of its bayonet fixing and only her palm, pressing down on it, kept it from falling on to the table. Using the thumb and index finger of her other hand, Beans grasped the bulb lower down towards its fixing and lifted it out of the lamp.

Ten minutes later she had another set of prints to add to her TOP SECRET file. Underneath the prints she wrote:

FINGERPRINTS (DAD'S)
FULL SET, PROBABLY FROM
LEFT HAND BECAUSE DAD IS
LEFT-HANDED. TAKEN FROM
BEDSIDE-LAMP LIGHT BULB.

Beans compared her dad's fingerprints to the print she'd recovered off the cigarette packet. There was no match—in fact, none of the prints came close. But to make sure, she'd have to find something with a set of prints from Dad's right hand. Beans went once more through the OPERATION GADGETMAN file. No new ideas sprung to mind. After that, all Beans wanted to do was sleep. It had been a long, long day and she'd be no good to her dad if she was too tired to think. After cleaning her teeth and going to kiss her gran good-night, Beans went back to her room and fell into bed, hugging her OPERATION GADGETMAN folder to her.

*　　　*　　　*

Saturday morning turned out to be another beautifully warm day, with hardly a cloud in the sky. Beans quickly had her shower and got dressed. She had a lot to do today and she didn't want to waste a second of it.

It was only when Beans came out of the shower that she realized what it was that had been bothering her ever since she set foot out of her bedroom. The landing was tidy! No capacitors, no cathodes, no insulating tape— nothing on the landing carpet for her to pick her way through on her way to her bathroom. Gran had been busy! Pausing on the landing, a horrible thought entered Beans's head. She ran to her dad's room.

Spotless!

You could actually see the carpet, the bed was tidy, and all the knick-knacks that had littered the floor were now in a box in the corner of the room.

'On no!' Beans groaned.

How was she going to get a set of prints from Dad's right hand now? She wouldn't know which prints were Gran's and which ones were Dad's. She could always finger-print Gran—but no . . . Gran would never allow it!

I'm going to end up fingerprinting the whole street at this rate,' Beans mumbled with annoyance.

She looked around the bedroom again. Dad wouldn't be able to find a thing in all this neatness! He was going to hit the ceiling when he saw it.

'But you *will* see it, Dad,' Beans whispered. And she went downstairs.

As she suspected, the whole house was spotless. Every surface had been wiped and dusted and vacuum-cleaned, every stray nut and bolt had been put away.

It's like being in a completely different house, Beans thought, as she sat down for her breakfast.

Gran joined her, a bowl of wheat flakes in hot milk in front of her. Beans wrinkled up her nose at it. Thank goodness Gran didn't insist on her having to eat the same thing for breakfast.

'I hardly slept a wink,' Gran sighed. She lifted her spoon up to her mouth before letting the spoon drop with a clatter back into the bowl. She pushed her breakfast away, eyeing it with distaste. Surprised, Beans looked at Gran.

'I'm not hungry,' Gran said tersely.

Beans bent her head. She studied her sausages and beans on toast. She wasn't hungry either.

'He'll be all right, Beatrice,' Gran said. Beans looked up. Her gran was smiling at her. Beans smiled back.

Just at that moment, the doorbell rang.

'Now who can that be so early in the morning?' Gran's eyebrows almost met in the middle as she frowned.

She stood up and went to answer the door. Beans followed her.The silhouette she could see through the glass panel in the front door looked familiar. Gran opened the door. It was Detective Warner. He had on navy-blue cords and a light blue shirt and the same leather jacket as he had worn the day before.

'Hello. I'm sorry to bother you. You must be Mrs Conran, Beans's grandmother?' Detective Warner said.

'That's right. Can I help you?' Gran frowned.

'I'm Detective Warner.We spoke on the phone yesterday. I wonder if I might come in? I'd like a word with Beans,' the detective said.

'You've found Dad?' Beans asked eagerly.

'Er . . . not as such. That's what I wanted to talk to you about.' Detective Warner craned his neck to see past Gran. 'Beans, I wanted to talk to you about the induction oscillator.'

'You haven't found my son?' Gran questioned. 'Just what are you police doing? Sitting down drinking tea and playing cards whilst my son could be anywhere, in any condition.'

'We're doing everything we can, madam. If I could just come in . .' said Detective Warner.

Gran took a deep breath. 'Yes, of course. I'm sorry,' she sighed. 'This way.'

Beans led the way into the sitting-room. Gran stood by the door as Detective Warner stood in front of Beans.

'Beans, did you find any information on the induction oscillator?' he asked.

'Not yet,' Beans dismissed. 'What about Dad? Have you found out anything yet?'

'No, I'm afraid not. We still have him listed as missing,' Detective Warner said.

'Missing?' Gran said from behind the detective. 'Cats go missing. Umbrellas go missing. My son has been abducted.'

'Yes, of course, Mrs Conran,' the detective soothed.

'Hhmm!' Gran folded her arms across her chest.'

Detective Warner turned to Beans again. 'I was passing this way so I just popped in on the off chance that you might have found some written details about the induction oscillator,' Detective Warner said. 'It's important that we take custody of all your father's notes and blueprints on his invention as soon as possible—assuming, of course, that your father doesn't tell his abductors what they want to know.'

'Never,' Beans and Gran spoke in unison.

'Hhmm! Have the kidnappers been in touch?' asked Detective Warner.

Beans shook her head. 'We haven't heard a thing, have we, Gran?' she replied. 'But the kidnappers have what they want. They've got Dad and his induction oscillator. Why should they want to get in touch with me or Gran?'

'We're working on a few theories,' was all Detective Warner would say. 'Beans, I want you to contact me if you hear anything from your dad or his kidnappers. Don't forget. And if you find any information on the oscillator, get in touch immediately. You have my phone number. Don't forget now'

'I won't forget,' Beans nodded. 'Er . . . Detective Warner, have the police told other banks or building societies about Dad's oscillator?'

'No. We wanted to get more information about it or speak to your father first,' Detective Warner frowned. 'Why?'

'No reason. Just wondered.' Beans shrugged.

Gran escorted the policeman to the door. Beans stayed where she was. She couldn't believe that Dad would tell his kidnappers a thing about the oscillator—so what would they do then? Would they hurt him? Gran walked back into the sitting-room.

'Gran . . . Gran, I'm frightened,' Beans admitted with a whisper.

Her gran came over to her, hugging her tightly. 'So am I, Beans,' Gran said. 'So am I!'

Chapter Eight

The Giveaway

'I want to go to the building society,' Beans announced. 'It suddenly occurred to me this morning that if only the building society and the police are supposed to know about Dad's induction oscillator, then how did the kidnappers find out about it?'

'Good point,' Ann said, surprised.

'I thought so!' Beans grinned. 'So I thought I'd have a word with the building society manager to see if he or she spoke to any reporters or told any other banks or building societies. I know the police haven't.'

'Let's get down there then,' said Louisa firmly.

Ann and Louisa had arrived together only a few minutes before. Beans had waited for them by her gate. She was eager to be off and doing things. Sitting around the house gave her too much time to think.

The twenty-minute bus journey from Beans's house to the building society was spent discussing the cigarette packet and the fingerprints Beans had acquired the previous night. The bus crawled along. Beans *burned* to speak to the building society manager. She was closer to finding the kidnappers, she just knew it. If she could find out what had put the kidnappers on to Dad, then she'd be on their trail. There had to be people that someone at Dad's building society had told. That was the only explanation.

But once they were actually in front of the building society, Beans wasn't sure what to do next.

'Well, there it is,' she said nervously. 'I've never actually been inside it before.'

'We can't do anything from out here,' Louisa said. 'We'd better go in.'

They walked inside. After the warmth and sunshine outside, it was like walking into a fridge. Beans shivered. If that was air conditioning then she'd rather do without it!

'We'd better join the queue at the enquiries desk,' Louisa suggested. Louisa led the way and they all stood in the queue together. Ann said what they were all thinking.

'Will they let three girls speak to the manager?' she asked.

'We'll insist,' Beans said firmly.

Ann grinned at Beans. Beans smiled back. She hadn't come this far to be turned away now.

The queue moved just as slowly as the bus had done. Beans hated all this waiting around. She wanted to be *doing* something. At last they reached the front of the queue.

'Excuse me,' Beans began. 'I'd like . . .

to . . speak . . .' Her voice trailed off altogether.

'Is something wrong? Can I help you?' the male cashier behind the glass window asked.

Ann and Louisa looked at Beans, wondering what was the matter.

'Look!' Beans pointed past the cashier to where the other workers in the building society sat at their desks.

'What?' Louisa frowned.

'Over there. That man. *Look!*' Beans said urgently.

Ann and Louisa looked over in the direction of Beans's pointing finger. A bearded man sat at his desk, which was piled high with papers and filing trays. His head was bent. In his left hand he held a sheet of paper, which he carefully examined. His right hand was drumming on his table as he read.

'What about him?' Ann asked.

'Can I help you? You're holding up the queue,' the cashier said patiently.

'Oh, er . . . that man over there—he was the one who helped me before but I can't remember his name,' Beans said.

The cashier turned around. 'Who? Lucas?'

'Lucas. That was his name.' Beans nodded quickly. 'He helped me out with a query I had about opening an account at this building society.'

'Are you sure it was Lucas?' the cashier turned to face Beans, a frown on his face. 'I think you've made a mistake. Lucas is the correspondence clerk.'

'What does a correspondence clerk do?' Beans asked eagerly.

'Opens letters and things,' Louisa butted in.

'That's right. He makes sure that all the letters go to the appropriate person or department. And he handles all outgoing post. Why?' asked the cashier.

'Look, dear, I *am* in a hurry.' From behind them in the queue, an elderly woman with grey-white hair rapped Beans on the shoulder.

'Won't be long. Promise.' Beans turned back to the cashier. 'Do all incoming letters and packets and stuff go through him first?'

'Yes.' The cashier nodded.

'I'm sure he's the one that I was talking to,' Beans insisted. 'His last name is . . . is Deacon.'

'No, it's not. It's Moynahan,' the cashier said. 'Lucas! LUCAS! This girl says that . . .'

'NO! DON'T!' Beans said.

But she was too late.

Lucas Moynahan looked up and across to the cashier. Then he saw Beans. She saw him start slightly and knew that he recognized her, just as she had recognized him. The next moment seemed to last forever as they regarded each other. Lucas stood up slowly, his eyes narrowed.

'No, it wasn't him after all,' Beans said quickly. 'Sorry. I made a mistake. Come on, you two.'

Beans grabbed Louisa and Ann and pulled them out of the queue.

'What was that all about?' Ann frowned as they headed outside.

The sudden sunlight made Beans blink rapidly. She licked her lips.

'Do you two remember that blue Escort parked opposite my house yesterday afternoon? I pointed it out—remember?'

'Yeah! So?' Ann asked.

'That was the driver,' Beans replied. 'Lucas Moynahan was the driver.'

Louisa and Ann stared at her.

'He couldn't have been,' Louisa said. 'Are you sure?'

'I'm positive. That was him,' Beans said. 'He was wearing sunglasses yesterday, but I still recognize him.'

'What was he doing outside your house then?' Ann asked.

Beans shrugged. 'I don't know. But it's a bit of a coincidence that he was parked outside my house and now we find out that he works at Dad's very same building society. I bet he knows something about Dad's letter and the money. The only trouble is, that twerp of a cashier called out to him and Lucas saw me.' Beans couldn't keep her voice from trembling slightly. She wasn't sure if it shook from fear or a strange kind of excitement. Maybe it was both.

'What should we do?' Ann asked.

Beans glanced down at her watch.

'Well, the building society closes in ten minutes. They're only open half day today,' Beans said, thinking hard. 'So what we need to do is wait for that Lucas bloke to come out. Then one of us will have to follow him to see where he goes. We need to know where he lives.'

'Let me tail him!' Ann pleaded. 'I read all about tailing suspects in your dad's instruction book last night.'

'I don't know. It might be dangerous. Very dangerous,' said Beans. 'Only one of us should follow Lucas Moynahan. Two or three of us would be too easy to spot. If anyone does it, it should be me.'

'But he knows who you are and what you look like,' Ann argued. 'Besides, Beans, you can't do everything yourself.'

'I know that, Ann—and thanks for offering, but this is serious. The men who kidnapped my dad did it because they were after money and they reckoned Dad's induction oscillator was the way to get it.Those sort of people don't go round you if you get in their way, they run straight over you. And I'd never forgive myself if anything happened to you either of you.'

Ann reached out and placed a hand on Beans's arm.

'Beans,' Ann began. 'I know I may sound like I'm not taking this seriously, but I promise I am. Your dad's been kidnapped and I want to do everything I can to help. I also know it's dangerous, so don't worry—I intend to be very, *very* careful following our Mr Moynahan.'

'Of course, we may not have to follow him,' Louisa interrupted. 'We could try looking up his name, address and phone number in a telephone directory.'

Beans and Ann stared at Louisa before they all started grinning.

'I do have good ideas *sometimes*,' Louisa said.

'I'd never have thought of anything so simple!' admitted Beans. 'All right then, Ann—you win. You can wait here in case our man leaves early and doesn't go home. Louisa and I will head for the nearest phone box to check him out. We'll be right back.'

'Hang on half a sec!' Louisa pulled an enthusiastic Beans back when she would have sprinted off. 'We need a back-up plan for if Lucas Moynahan *does* decide to leave before we get back.'

'True!' Beans agreed dryly. 'Let me think. What would Dad suggest at a time like this . . . ? Well . . . if Lucas leaves in a car, then there's not an awful lot Ann can do. So she can wait here for us. Agreed?'

Ann nodded. 'Agreed.'

'If he goes to a bus stop or walks off somewhere then follow him, but *be careful* and don't go too far out of town,' Louisa added.

'If you aren't here when we get back . . . we'll head back to my home . . . and wait for you to call us there,' Beans said slowly. 'Then we'll come out to join you wherever you are. The most important thing, though, is to take care. At the first sign of trouble, or if you're detected—run!'

'Dead right!' Ann snorted. 'I don't

need to be told that!'

And with that they separated.

The nearest phone kiosk was in the shopping precinct. Beans and Louisa weren't keen on losing sight of Ann, but they had no choice. Beans opened the telephone directory and began to flick through its pages.

'Yaahoo! He's here!' she shouted, before remembering where she was.

Moynahan, L. Mrs
          47 Upper Crescent,
          Cleevesdon
          5927070

Moynahan, Lucas
          Oak House,
          Berryfield,
          Nr Cleevesdon
          2694252

'Louisa, have you got a pen?' Beans asked.

'Yeah, here you are,' Louisa said excitedly.

She handed it over, and Beans wrote the address and phone number down on the back of her hand.

'I would have brought my spy kit along, but I thought it'd get in the way,' Beans said.

'Same here. I'm sorry I didn't now,' Louisa said.

Beans studied what she had written. 'Oak House, Berryfield . . . He lives quite a way out.'

'The perfect place to keep someone you've snatched,' Louisa said. 'An out-of-the-way spot, surrounded by fields and trees . . .'

'And not too many nosy neighbours,' Beans finished. 'Come on. Let's get back to Ann.'

'Hang on. How about if we tried phoning his home first?' Louisa suggested. 'We know from your dad's letter that there's at least one other man involved in all this somewhere. Maybe the second man is at Lucas Moynahan's house right this second.'

'But what good will phoning him up do?' Beans asked.

Louisa shrugged. 'We'll know for definite if another person is there. If someone *is* there, tell them you're from a charity or something, but in the meantime listen out to see if you can hear any background noises. You might even hear your dad.'

'It's a bit unlikely,' Beans said doubtfully.

'But it's worth a try. You've got nothing to lose,' Louisa said.

And Beans couldn't argue with that. After dialling the number, she held the phone between her right ear and Louisa's left. It had barely rung once before the phone at the other end was picked up.

'For God's sake, Lucas, I'm moving as fast as I can. Stop phoning me. You're panicking.' The man's voice at the other end of the line was angry, impatient.

Beans's heart leapt up to her throat. She struggled to find something to say. The words of the man at the other end of the line had thrown her.

'Hello. I'm from . . . I'm from . . .' Beans's voice dried up. Her mind went blank. The silence at the other end of the line was deafening.

'Who is that?' the man said at last,

the wariness in his voice crackling down the phone.

Louisa nodded frantically at Beans. 'Go on!' she mouthed.

Beans's mouth was bone dry, her tongue stuck to her palette. She swallowed hard, then swallowed again. It didn't help.

'Can I . . . can I speak to M-Mr Conran, please?' Beans's whispered words came out in a rush. At the other end of the phone, the man gasped.

'Who is this? *Who is this?*' he asked furiously.

Then the phone was slammed down.

Chapter Nine

That Was Dad!

'Beans, are you crazy? What did you say that for?' Louisa asked, appalled.

Beans stared at the receiver in her hand. The continuous purr it made, showing that the connection had been broken, mocked her.

'Beans!' snapped Louisa.

'It was your idea to phone in the first place,' Beans argued.

'I never told you to ask *that*,' Louisa

fumed. Now they're on to us. They know we think your dad is there.'

'It . . . it just slipped out,' Beans said miserably. 'Besides, they don't know it was me.'

'Talk sense. Who else would it be?' said Louisa.

Deep down, Beans was just as shocked as Louisa. She hadn't meant to ask that at all. 'It's just that . . that suddenly all · I could see was Dad locked up or tied up and all for a stupid gadget. He's *there*! I just know he's there. I can *feel* it.'

'Feel it, my left eyeball!' Louisa scoffed. 'Beans, you need more proof than feelings. Detective Warner isn't interested in your feelings. Suppose you got it wrong? Suppose that was Lucas Moynahan's dad or brother or something and they have nothing to do with your dad?'

'Yeah, but the man on the phone complained that Lucas has been phoning him a lot. I bet that was after he saw me in the building society,' Beans tried to defend herself.

'That doesn't prove anything. Lucas

might have been phoning up all the time to make sure his lunch was ready when he got home,' Louisa said.

Crestfallen, Beans nodded.

'And supposing, just supposing, you're right. What if Lucas Moynahan and the man you just spoke to *are* somehow involved in your dad's kidnapping? All you've done now is tip them off,' Louisa said.

'I was stupid, wasn't I?' Beans said glumly.

'Yes, you were,' Louisa agreed immediately. 'Come on, let's get back to Ann.'

As they walked back, Beans said, 'I'm sure I'm right about Lucas Moynahan though. He would have been the first one at the building society to read Dad's letter. As soon as I get home I think I'd better give Detective Warner a call.'

'You're certain Moynahan's the one you saw outside your house?' Louisa asked. 'As I remember, the man you saw in the Escort had on sunglasses . . .'

'It *was* him,' Beans replied immediately. 'I recognized him at once.

He also has this habit of drumming his fingers. He was drumming his fingers on the steering wheel when I saw him the first time, and he was drumming his fingers on the table just now.'

'Are you sure you didn't see the drumming fingers and the beard and put two and two together to make three and three-quarters?' Louisa asked.

'No, I didn't. It was him. I know it was. Besides, you didn't see the way he looked at me. He recognized me all right,' Beans retorted.

The rest of the short walk back to Ann was carried out in silence. Beans glanced up at the blue sky, shading her eyes from the dazzling sun. It was going to be a scorcher. Was Dad somewhere where he could, see it . . . ? Feel it . . . ?

They reached the line of cars opposite the building society where they'd left Ann.

She wasn't there . . .

'Ann . . .' Louisa called out nervously.

Beans looked around quickly, hoping Ann was still in sight. She wasn't.

'Stay there,' Louisa ordered.

Before Beans could argue, Louisa crossed the road and went up to the building society. Bean's heart moved up to her mouth as she watched Louisa try to push open the front doors. A tall, slim woman with black hair appeared almost immediately and said something to Louisa through the glass doors. Louisa spoke back. Licking her lips, Beans glanced up and down the main road, wondering if she should cross it to be with Louisa. As Beans watched, the woman unbolted the doors and spoke to Louisa directly.

Just when Beans thought she'd have to join her friend or die of curiosity, she saw Louisa smile and thank the woman from the building society before turning to recross the road.

'What happened? What did you say to her? What did she say to you?' Beans was all questions.

'They closed over five minutes ago and our man Moynahan was out the door about two seconds afterwards,' Louisa filled in. 'I said he was supposed to be having dinner with us later and Mum had sent me with a message for him.'

'So Ann must have followed him,' Beans said nervously. 'I hope she's all right.'

'I'm fine.' Ann's voice behind them made both Beans and Louisa jump.

'Ann! Where were you? I was beginning to get worried.'

'I followed what's-his-face to the car park around the corner,' Ann said. 'He got into his car—*his blue Ford Escort car*—and drove off, so I couldn't follow him.'

'I *knew* it was the same guy. I knew it!' Beans hopped up and down. 'He *was* parked outside my house yesterday. Ann, he didn't see you, did he?'

'Are you kidding?' Ann said, her hands on her hips. 'Of course he didn't see me. I've read your dad's book!'

'I'm certain now that he's involved in Dad's kidnapping—absolutely certain.' Beans's eyes narrowed.

'That's all very well, but what's our next move?' Louisa said, bursting Beans's bubble by injecting a practical note into the conversation.

Beans chewed her bottom lip for a moment. 'We visit Lucas Moynahan at his house. We see if my dad's there.'

'You got his address? More spying! Yes!' Ann waved her arms above her head.

'Maybe now would be a good time to call Detective Warner?' Louisa suggested.

'Why? We don't have any more evidence or information than we did yesterday,' Beans argued. 'I reckon we should call him after we've been to Moynahan's house. If we manage to pick up some clues there, then we'll definitely phone him.'

'Let's hope that when we want to go to the police, we haven't left it too late,' Louisa muttered.

Beans looked at her but said nothing.

They headed for the bus stop.

I wonder if Ann and Louisa feel as nervous as I do? Beans thought. What would she do if Dad was in Lucas Moynahan's house? What would happen then? How would they rescue him?

119

*　　*　　*

Oak House was indeed well hidden. Miles out of town, you had to turn up an unmarked side track which was very easy to miss, overgrown as it was with brambles and bushes which grew higher than Beans's waist. It was only thanks to the bus driver's instructions that Beans and her friends didn't miss the turning altogether. The entangled leaves on the trees above them were an all-enveloping cloak, deadening the light from the afternoon sun and flattening sound.They could hear one or two birds chirping and lazy buzzing sounds from distant insects, but even those noises were quiet and subdued.

'Do you think Lucas came back here?' Ann whispered.

Louisa shrugged as Beans said, 'Shush!'

They carried on walking. The ground under their feet was baked hard, making the going very tiring. Beans studied the path for tyre marks or other potential clues, but the rock-solid earth held nothing but the faintest impressions.

'Keep your eyes and ears open for clues, everyone,' Beans whispered.

'Shush!' Ann said. 'What's that noise?'

They all stood absolutely still and listened.

'It's a car. A car's coming!' said Beans. 'Get back!' Louisa ordered. 'It might be Lucas.'

The track lay before and behind them. To the sides lay brambles and bushes and stinging nettles, with dense trees behind that. They each stood there, none of them keen to scramble through the thick undergrowth. The unmistakable sound of a car engine was getting closer.

'Beans, Louisa . . .' Ann said desperately. 'What do we do?'

'We've got no choice,' Beans said. 'Come on!'

They waded through the bushes and brambles before squatting down, out of sight.

'I can't believe I'm doing this,'

Louisa muttered. 'I dread to think what I'm standing in.'

'Shush!' the other two girls glared at her.

The car came closer and closer. From around the bend just up ahead, the blue Ford Escort appeared unexpectedly quickly and drove straight towards them. There, in the driver's seat, was Lucas Moynahan. But Lucas wasn't the only one in the car.

Beans jumped up. 'Dad . . . DAD!' she screamed as the car roared past them.

'What?' Ann said.

'My dad's in that car!' Beans started running after the Escort, which was speeding away from them. Two men sat in the back seat and one of them was her dad. He turned his head, his expression frantic as he mouthed words Beans couldn't hear. Dad! Dad was in there. So close . . .'

Suddenly, the car screeched to a halt. Beans froze.

'Beans . . . Beans, come back!' Louisa ran forward and grabbed her by the arm.

One of the Escort doors opened. Lucas Moynahan got out of the car.

'Come back, you two!' Ann cried out. 'They're after us.'

Beans hesitated for only a second. She pelted back to Ann and all three of them dived for cover into the bushes, scrambling to get as far away from Lucas as possible.

'Come back here!'

They heard Lucas's furious voice call after them. If anything, his voice made them scramble faster and further away from him. Beans pointed to the right and they veered off in that direction, roots and brambles tearing at their clothes, scratching at their faces.

'Keep still, everyone!' Louisa hissed.

They each froze. The crunch of Lucas's angry footsteps through the undergrowth made Beans's stomach churn with fright.

'BEANS, THEY'RE AFTER YOU! DON'T LET THEM CATCH YOU. DON'T TRUST . . .' Beans's dad's words were abruptly stifled.

Beans raised her head. 'Dad . . .' she mouthed. She wanted to shout out to

123

him, run to him a feeling so strong she could almost reach out and touch it. But she couldn't.

She couldn't.

Beans stared through the brambles and bushes as if all she had to do was stare hard enough and they would disappear out of her way and she would see her father.

The footsteps were getting closer. All three girls lowered their heads. Ann put her hands over her ears. Lucas Moynahan might be gaining on them, but she didn't have to listen to it!

A few more steps and he'll be tripping over us, Beans thought desperately.

'Lucas, get back here!' the furious voice of Lucas's accomplice commanded. 'Don't be an idiot.'

'Those girls are somewhere around here,' Lucas called back.

Beans held her breath. Lucas was close enough for her to reach out and touch his foot.

'Leave them! We don't need them,' the accomplice shouted impatiently.

'We need her. She can persuade her

father to give us what we want then we can blow,' Lucas called back. 'We should have grabbed her in the beginning when I said so. I've had enough of both of them messing me about. I'd like to wring that girl's neck.'

Beans's breath caught in her throat. She stared at Lucas's feet, her eyes, her whole body, filled with terror.

They were after her as well now . . .

'We'll get her later. Come on. We've got to go,' the accomplice said.

'Don't worry, Beatrice Conran—I'll get you . . .' Lucas hissed to himself.

Slowly, reluctantly, Lucas headed back to his car. The girls heard angry mutterings from the two kidnappers, but were too far away to make out the words. Ann, Louisa and Beans didn't move; they didn't even breathe until they heard the car engine start up and the car being driven away. Louisa moved to stand up.

'Not yet,' Beans whispered quickly. 'It might be a trick. One of them might still be here, waiting for us to raise our heads.'

'It's all right for you two. I've got a

skirt on,' Louisa grumbled.

What on earth did you wear a skirt for?' Ann hissed.

'Because no-one told me I'd be crawling on my hands and knees through the countryside, that's why!' Louisa snapped, her voice still a whisper. 'I hate getting dirty . . .'

'At least you didn't have a twig sticking up your left nostril the entire time, whilst Lucas Moynahan was two centimetres away from you . . .' Ann interrupted.

'Shush!' Beans ordered.

They waited a couple of minutes but could hear nothing but birds chirping and insects buzzing. From somewhere far away, a dog barked.

'Ann, you crawl off over there,' Beans pointed to the left. 'I'll crawl over to the right. Then I'll stand up and see if they've gone.'

'Why can't we stick together?' Louisa protested.

'Because if they *are* still here, we'll be easier to catch if we stick together. If we split up then they're unlikely to get all three of us,' Beans whispered.

'The one or two remaining can then go straight to the police and tell Detective Warner what happened.'

Reluctantly, Louisa agreed that the plan made sense. They separated, Ann crawling off on her stomach in one direction, Beans heading in the other. Beans watched the second hand of her watch count down another minute before she slowly raised her head then stood up, ready to sprint off at the first sign of Lucas or the other kidnapper. There was no-one there. Beans took a good look around.

'Ann, Louisa, you can stand up now. We're alone.' Beans didn't know whether to be glad or disappointed.

But at least her dad was all right. Beans hugged that knowledge to her like a winter coat. Dad had spoken to her. He was all right so far. Slowly, the other two girls stood up.

'Just look at my skirt and blouse. They're ruined!' Louisa howled as she looked down at the green-and-brown stains on her clothes.

'Never mind your clothes,' Ann dismissed. 'Those stains will wash out.'

'I'm not thinking of that. I'm thinking about what my mum and dad are going to say when they see them,' Louisa retorted. 'Mum's going to go through the roof and hit the chimney stack!'

Ann walked over to Beans, ignoring Louisa. 'That was definitely your dad, Beans. I saw him too,' she said.

'I've had enough of playing amateur spy!' Louisa marched over to her friends. 'It's time we got the police in on this.'

'I agree,' Beans said. 'Now that we all know Lucas Moynahan is one of the kidnappers, the police should have no trouble from here on in.'

Chapter Ten

Sergeant Paxman

'You're certain the driver was Lucas Moynahan?' Detective Warner asked over the phone.

Beans wanted to bang the phone down and keep banging it until Detective Warner's ears popped! How many more times was he going to ask the same question?

'Yes, I am positive. Certain. Sure. It was him,' Beans said with thinly disguised impatience. 'I saw him in my dad's building society earlier today. We looked up his address and went over there. Only we were too late. He was driving off—with my dad in the back seat of his car.'

Ann nodded approval. 'You tell him.'

'Was there anyone else in the car besides your dad and Lucas Moynahan?'

Beans could hear the wary frown in Detective Warner's voice.

'Yeah, there was the other man but I didn't get a good look at him,' Beans admitted. 'I was so surprised and happy to see Dad that I didn't look at anyone else after that.'

'You say your friends Louisa and Ann were with you?' the detective asked.

Beans nodded. 'That's right.'

'Did they see the third man? Can either of them describe him?'

'Hang on. I'll ask,' Beans said. She turned to Louisa and Ann, who were standing right in front of her. 'Can either of you describe the man who was sitting next to Dad in the car?'

Ann shook her head. 'I was too busy staring at your dad and trying to memorise the licence number of the car.'

Louisa shook her head. 'I was doing the same as Ann. I only noticed your dad. Sorry. I did notice that the third man had sunglasses on, but that's all, I'm afraid.'

Beans repeated what had been said to Detective Warner.

'Does Ann still remember the licence number?' Detective Warner asked.

Beans handed over the telephone. 'He wants to know the licence number of the car,' she whispered.

Ann took the receiver. 'Hello? Detective Warner? It was . . . er . . . just a minute. It was . . . E391RP something. I can't remember the last letter, but I'm sure the rest is right. Yeah . . . Thanks . . . Yes, she's here.' Ann handed the phone back to Beans.

'Detective Warner, you have the kidnapper's name. Surely the licence number isn't that necessary?' Beans said at once.

131

'It all helps,' Detective Warner replied. 'Is there anything else you want to tell me, Beans?'

'No, I don't think so,' Beans said slowly. 'I gave you Lucas Moynahan's address, but I wouldn't have thought he'd go back there. You've got his car licence-plate number from Ann, and we each saw my dad. I told you what happened.'

'Are you at home now?' Detective Warner asked.

'Yes,' Beans replied. 'We hopped on a passing bus and came straight home. We didn't want to risk running across the kidnappers again, in case they decided to finish what they'd started.'

'Good. Very wise. Now, listen carefully, Beans. I'm going to be busy co-ordinating the setting up of roadblocks throughout the county, and I'll be arranging garage checks and searches of any and all car parks where Lucas Moynahan might try to hide his car,' said Detective Warner. 'I want you to stay at home and wait for word from me. I shall be around either later this evening or first thing tomorrow morning to tell you how the search for your father is going. Do you understand?'

'Yes.' Beans frowned at the phone. 'But isn't there something I can do . . . ?'

'The best thing you can do is stay at home,' Detective Warner interrupted. 'Is your gran there now?'

'No, she's gone shopping. But she should be at home soon, and my friends are here too,' Beans replied.

'What about tomorrow morning? Will your gran and your friends be around then?'

'Well, Gran always goes to church on Sunday morning,' Beans said. 'And I wouldn't have thought Ann and Louisa would be around tomorrow. Not until the afternoon, at any rate.'

'Good. Good,' Detective Warner said briskly. 'I have a lot to sort out today so it'll probably be tomorrow before I can call on you to tell you of our progress. You did very well in identifying one of the kidnappers, but now it's time to leave it to the professionals.'

'If you say so,' Beans sniffed.

133

The professionals hadn't done much so far!

'I insist,' Detective Warner said sternly. 'We'll see you tomorrow. And in the meantime, it's most important that you search out information about your dad's induction oscillator.'

'OK. I'll search tonight,' Beans said.

She wondered why Detective Warner kept harping on about the induction oscillator. Surely, finding Dad was far more important than knowing how the induction oscillator worked?

The detective put down the phone.

'So what did he say?' Ann asked eagerly. 'Is he going to send someone round for our statements?'

'No,' Beans shook her head. 'He said he'd come round tomorrow to tell me what progress he's made.'

'No statements!' Ann said, deeply disappointed.

'Wasn't he concerned that Lucas said he wanted to use you to get at your dad?' Louisa asked, surprised.

'It doesn't seem like it. I told him that obviously Dad hasn't told the kidnappers how his gadget works yet, so they want to use me to force Dad's hand. I told him all that.' Beans shrugged. She hoped she didn't look too worried. She didn't want to scare her friends. She was more than scared enough for all of them. Would Lucas and the other kidnapper really be after her? What would they do? Force their way into the house? Wait until she went to school on Monday? What? Beans felt sick.

'So what did he say?' Louisa asked.

'Not a lot. He said he'd be round tomorrow,' Beans repeated.

'He's not going to send someone round to protect you?' Ann asked, aghast.

'I can protect myself,' Beans said firmly.

'It's the job of the police to protect you,' Louisa said with disgust. 'It's not up to you to do it yourself.'

'I can't exactly go round to the police station and drag Detective Warner back here by force, can I?' Beans said crossly.

Nothing had gone right today, and to be so close to Dad actually to hear his voice only to lose him again, was frustrating to say the very least.

There was the sound of a key turning and the front door opened. Gran struggled over the threshold with two heavy shopping bags.

'Gran! Let me help you with that,' Beans said at once, leaping forward to take the shopping.

'My goodness! Where have you three been?' Gran asked. 'You look like you've been rolling backwards and forwards in green paint and mud.'

'You're not far wrong,' Ann laughed.

'I can't send you home like that,' Gran said, scandalized.

Louisa quickly whispered something in Ann's ear. Ann nodded. They both approached Gran, broad smiles on their faces.

'That's just what we wanted to talk to you about, Mrs Conran,' Ann said. 'Beans has asked us to spend the night here, but we wanted to ask your permission. If you have no objections, we thought you could phone up our parents and tell them that it's OK with you if we stay here.'

Beans frowned at Ann. Where had she got that story from?

Gran smiled. 'I'd be happy to phone your parents. Beans, you unpack the shopping whilst I sort this out.'

Beans took the shopping into the kitchen, leaving Gran to phone first Louisa's then Ann's parents. Fifteen minutes later, when Beans had just packed away the last item—a packet of quick-cook macaroni—Louisa, Ann and her gran all appeared in the kitchen.

'That's all settled then,' Gran smiled. 'Now then, you three. Off with those dirty things and I'll throw them in the washing machine. Beans, go upstairs with your friends and give them some of your clean clothes.'

'And there I was, about to give them my dirty ones out of the linen basket,' Beans muttered.

'I heard that, madam!' said Gran.

Laughing, the three girls ran upstairs and into Beans's bedroom. Beans closed the door carefully behind her before turning to Louisa and Ann.

'Now you two can tell me just what

137

all that was about downstairs,' Beans ordered. 'Why the sudden rush to spend the night?'

'Because I think your dad's kidnappers are out to get you as well, even if Detective Warner doesn't,' Louisa answered. 'And there's no way we're going to leave you alone tonight so that they *can* get you.'

'Dead right!' Ann smiled. Her smile faded. 'But what can we do?'

'Plenty,' Louisa said. 'We'll set up some traps and alarms in the house, just in case the kidnappers should try anything funny.'

'What sort of traps?' Beans asked suspiciously. 'I don't want to set up anything that could hurt my gran. And besides, how can we set up alarms that Gran won't set off?'

'Don't worry. I've got a plan,' Louisa smiled.

It was lucky for Beans and her friends that there was nothing on the telly that Gran wanted to watch. She decided to go to bed early, leaving the house free and clear for Beans and Louisa and Ann.

Following Louisa's instructions, they raided the kitchen and the airing cupboard and the cupboard in the front room where Dad kept all his stationery. Beans's bedroom took half an hour to prepare, but at last it was ready.

A plethora of coat hangers hung on the door handle and behind the door on the dressing-gown hook, ready to rattle if Beans's bedroom door was even looked at sideways. Tin cans were strewn on the carpet directly under her bedroom window. The curtains were partially drawn to hide the drawing pins littered across the window-sill. A frying pan was placed under either pillow on Beans's bed, and a rounders bat was placed behind the headboard. The only thing Beans wasn't too sure about was the cornflakes scattered around her bed.

'That's our alarm if the kidnappers get past the other traps,' Louisa said. 'They'll scrunch the cornflakes underfoot and the noise will wake us up.'

'But I'll get ants and mice in

here . . .' Bean protested.

'Would you rather have ants and mice or kidnappers?' Louisa asked. It was a close thing, but the ants and mice won.

'Gran's going to go nuclear if she sees all those cornflakes on the floor,' Beans muttered.

'We'll vacuum them up before she sees them,' Louisa promised.

'Hhmm!' Beans said, not totally convinced.

At last they went to bed. Louisa and Ann tossed a coin to see who would share Beans's double bed and who'd have to sleep on the lilo. Ann got the lilo, much to Louisa's relief.

They started watching the late-night movie on the telly in Beans's room, but it was a horror film and they all agreed that it was *not* the best time to watch something like that. Beans had to take a flying leap out of bed to unplug the telly, and another flying leap to get back into bed all to avoid the cornflakes. She reached up over her head to switch off the light. They all lay on their backs, listening to the dark silence in the house.

'I won't sleep a wink,' Beans whispered. She fingered the rounders bat. It felt smooth and reassuringly solid beneath her fingertips.

'Neither will I,' Louisa sighed.

'Nor me,' Ann joined in.

Ten minutes later, they were all fast asleep.

*　　　*　　　*

'Beatrice Teresa Conran! Just what have you been up to?'

Beans sat up, rubbing her eyes. 'Is it morning already?' she asked, surprised.

'Yes, it is morning. And you can just clean up this room and that means *every* cornflake removed from the carpet before you come down to breakfast,' Gran stormed.

Beans blinked. 'Yes, Gran.'

Ann sat up slowly. Louisa groaned and turned round, pulling the duvet over her head.

'So much for traps and alarms,' Beans said with disgust. She was *almost* disappointed.

An hour later, the tins and drawing pins and hangers were all back in their proper places. The cornflakes had been vacuumed up until the carpet looked like new.

'I'd still like to know what you three were up to.' Gran peered at her reflection in the hall mirror before straightening her hat.

'It was just an experiment, Gran,' Beans said for the umpteenth time.

'An experiment? AN EXPERIMENT! You and your father—God protect him—must learn to do your experiments out in the garden workroom and keep them out of the house,' Gran said. 'Mind you, I'm not surprised your dad works in this house sometimes, considering the state of his workroom! The door was just about to fall off its hinges. So untidy! I had to use your dad's tools to fix it this morning. Did that nice Detective Warner get in touch about your father whilst I was out shopping yesterday?'

'No, Gran. I'd tell you if he had,' Beans replied.

'I'm not so sure about that, Beatrice.'

142

Gran turned to wag a finger in Beans's direction. 'I know you don't want to upset me, so I wouldn't put it past you to keep bad news to yourself'

'Well, I'm not.'

'Just make sure you don't,' Gran sniffed. 'I'm not made of glass.'

'Yes, Gran . . . I mean, no, Gran,' Beans said.

'I just hope your dad's safe,' Gran muttered. 'If I didn't have you three girls to look after, I don't know what I'd do . . . All this worry.'

Beans was surprised, then she wondered *why* she was surprised. She was more like her gran than she had thought. They both had to *do* things to stop themselves from worrying too much. Only Gran's way of handling it was to keep busy with her shopping and dusting and cooking and cleaning and mending doors!

'I'm off to church now,' Gran said, straightening up. 'I want you three girls to behave yourselves. No more trying to plant cornflakes in the carpet!'

Louisa and Ann smiled.

'No, Gran,' Beans said.

143

Gran pulled her jacket down straight and headed out the door.

'Nag! Nag! Nag!' Beans muttered under her breath.

'I heard that, Beatrice!' Gran said. She popped her head round the door. 'If you three are seeking useful employment today, you can mow the lawn and water the flowers—in both the back and the front gardens. I started it this morning but didn't get a chance to finish. The side gate is open, so don't forget to lock it when you're all done. I don't want stray dogs wandering up our side path.' And with that, Gran closed the door firmly behind her.

'Your gran's dead ace,' Ann grinned. 'I like her!'

'Me, too,' Louisa agreed. 'She believes in coming straight to the point, doesn't she!'

'You two only like her because she's never inflicted her macaroni cheese on you,' Beans replied.

They wandered into the kitchen.

'Do you want us to help you with anything?' Louisa asked.

'I suppose we'd better start looking for any notes or drawings Dad might have made about his induction oscillator. Detective Warner has been pestering me about those for ages.'

'Where do we start?' Ann asked.

'Dad's workroom. Where else?' Beans said.

Beans thought that the search would take for ever, but Gran had beaten them to Dad's workroom and tidied that as well! Boxes of the same components were stacked neatly side by side against the wall. Screwdrivers were arranged in order of size on the worktable. Miscellaneous components were held in one large box. The broom leaned self-consciously against the wall by the window, and Dad's latest gadgets—the animal crunchies shaped like various animals or insects—were in a box by themselves.

To think that these little things could have caused all the trouble with our neighbour, Mr McKee, Beans thought.

She opened the drawers in her father's worktable and found all of his papers, filed neatly away. Gran again!

The notes on the induction oscillator had to be in there somewhere. Beans sighed. Working her way through all that lot would be a job and a half. The workroom was darker than it had been the day before. Beans glanced up. Gran had been up on the ladder to throw a tarpaulin over the hole in the roof. And as Gran said, she'd fixed the door so that it no longer swung haphazardly on its hinges, but closed properly. The workroom door's padlock and key had been placed on a shelf, just inside the door.

'I would never have recognized the place,' Ann whistled.

'Dad won't recognize it either,' Beans said. 'He's always been here before to stop Gran from tidying it up. I guess she couldn't help herself.'

'Here . . . Beans, isn't that your doorbell?' Louisa asked.

'I can't hear anything.' Beans turned her head to listen.

'Yes, it is,' Louisa said. 'There it goes again.'

Beans stared at her. 'How can you hear the doorbell from all the way out here? You must have ears like a Labrador!'

Louisa grinned They all went back inside the house. Louisa *was* right. There was someone at the door. Two people, in fact.

'Hello, Beans,' Detective Warner said. His piercing eyes seemed to look straight through her and her friends. 'Er . . . I've brought my sergeant with me today. This is Sergeant Paxman.'

Sergeant Paxman had his back to them as the detective spoke. At the introduction, he turned around slowly. Beans's breath caught in her throat for a moment. For a brief second Beans was sure she had seen Sergeant Paxman before. But that was impossible. He was a podgier man than Detective Warner, but strangely podgy.

Podgy in a squidgy way! Beans thought.

Sergeant Paxman was wearing sunglasses and his hair was gelled straight back off his head. His face had a sheen to it, which didn't surprise Beans.

He must be baking, Beans frowned

to herself.

Sergeant Paxman was wearing a zipped-up black leather jacket, and trousers which seemed to have a shape all of their own. If the trousers followed the shape of Sergeant Paxman's legs, then the sergeant had the most peculiarly shaped legs Beans had ever seen. She couldn't see Sergeant Paxman's face very well because he was standing just in front of the sun so that his face was shadowed.

'May we come in, Beans?' Detective Warner asked.

'Yes, of course?' Beans held open the door.

'I thought you were going to be alone this morning?' Detective Warner asked lightly, regarding Ann and Louisa.

'My friends stayed overnight,' Beans explained.

She watched Sergeant Paxman as he walked into the house out of the sun. It was strange, but the skin below his cheeks, around his mouth and his jaw-line, was noticeably lighter than the rest of his tanned face. Beans frowned.

She couldn't put her finger on it but there was something very strange about Sergeant Paxman. Something she didn't like—at all.

Chapter Eleven

Matching Fingerprints

'Have you any news about my dad?' Beans asked.

Detective Warner and Sergeant Paxman made themselves comfortable on the sofa. Sergeant Paxman picked up Beans's English workbook from where it was partially covered by a sofa cushion, and started flicking through it.

'We've got nothing concrete yet,' Detective Warner smiled. 'The car was found abandoned in the city centre, which doesn't give us much to go on, but we're still looking. What about you?'

'What about me?' Beans asked, puzzled.

'Did you find the blueprints for the induction oscillator or instructions for using it?'

Why did Detective Warner's smile remind Beans of an oil slick? Sergeant Paxman unzipped his jacket before pushing his sunglasses further up the bridge of his nose. He closed Beans's English notebook. He started drumming on the cover.

'I . . .' Beans froze.

She stared at Sergeant Paxman's fingers, drumming on her notebook.

Drumming. Drumming . . .

'Is something wrong, Beans?' Detective Warner frowned.

Beans looked at him. She clamped her teeth together, then forced herself to smile.

'No, of course not.' She was speaking too quickly. 'No, of course not,' she said again, making herself speak more slowly this time.

'So did you find what we're looking for?' the detective repeated. 'Any drawings or notes? Anything at all?'

'Not yet. But I'll find it today for sure. Can you go away and come back this evening for it?' Beans said.

'But Beans, what about all those papers in the workroom?' Louisa reminded her.

'Papers?' Detective Warner said quickly.

'Oh, they're not the ones you want,' Beans dismissed. 'Dad always keeps his notes and drawings on serious projects in his bedroom or in the attic. The papers in his workroom are details of his official Gadgetman spy kits.'

'Ah yes, the workroom. I'd like to take a look in there,' Detective Warner said.

'You've been in there before,' Beans said.

'No, I haven't,' the detective replied sharply. 'You're mistaken.'

'Oh . . I thought you had . . . I—I'd let you see it but . . . but Gran has padlocked the door and gone off to church with the key in her handbag,' Beans lied. 'Have you seen Dad's Gadgetman spy kits? They're going on sale at the end of the month. Would you like to see one? My kit is in my bedroom. Hang on a sec whilst . . .'

Detective Warner shook his head. 'No, we don't have time. So you think you'll find the papers on the induction oscillator today?'

'Yes, I'm sure of it,' Beans said. 'Could you wait there a moment, please?'

Beans pulled Ann and Louisa out of the sitting-room and into the kitchen.

'You two are not to say a word to those detectives. Not one word,' Beans whispered vehemently.

Beans ran round the kitchen, getting two glasses out of the cupboard. Ann and Louisa frowned at each other, totally baffled. Beans placed each glass in a saucer after cleaning them thoroughly with some kitchen towel first. Then she filled the glasses with fresh orange juice from the fridge.

'Is something wrong?' Detective Warner came to stand in the kitchen doorway, Sergeant Paxman behind him. Beans jumped.

'No . . . er . . .' I was just getting you both a drink. Some orange juice.' Beans smiled. She'd never found smiling so hard to do.

'No thanks,' Detective Warner said.

'Oh, but . . . but I've poured it out now' Beans held out the drinks by the saucers to the two detectives.

Detective Warner shrugged at Sergeant Paxman before taking the glass of orange juice. The sergeant took his drink. They both downed them in one before placing them back on the saucers.

'I . . . I'm sorry for the delay, but I only had a chance to really start looking for what you wanted this morning,' Beans said. 'Detective Warner, should I phone you when I find anything? At the same number as before?'

'Yes, do that,' the detective said.

'But like I said, I'm sure I'll find them later on today anyway,' Beans smiled.

'Fine,' said Detective Warner. 'We'll

see ourselves out.'

'Louisa, show them to the front door then.' Beans elbowed Louisa in the ribs to get her going.

Louisa frowned at Beans, but followed the two policemen out into the hall. Beans set down the glasses in their saucers carefully, one on either side of the hob.

'Warner.' Beans pointed to the now empty glass on the left. 'Paxman!' She pointed to the one on the right.

'Beans, what are . . . ?' Ann began.

'Ann, you can help me wash up these glasses,' Beans said, her voice louder than normal.

'Oh, all right,' Ann grumbled. 'But I wish you'd stop being so mysterious and tell me what's going on.'

Louisa came back into the kitchen.

'They've gone?' Beans whispered.

'Yes, of course,' said Louisa, surprised.

'You shut the front door behind them?'

Beans asked urgently.

Louisa nodded.

'ANN, DON'T YOU DARE

TOUCH THAT GLASS!' Beans screamed.

Ann's arm froze, just as her hand was about to pick up the now-empty glass used by one of the policemen.

'You just told me to help you wash up,' Ann said, annoyed.

'That was for *their* benefit, not yours,' Beans said. 'Wait here, you two. I'm just going to get my spy kit, and for goodness sake don't touch those glasses.'

'What's wrong with her?' Ann asked Louisa as Beans raced up the stairs.

'Don't ask me.' Louisa shrugged. 'She was fine until those two policemen arrived. Mind you, there was something weird about that sergeant. He didn't say much, did he? And . . .'

They heard Beans charge downstairs. She ran full pelt into the kitchen, spy-kit briefcase in one hand, OPERATION GADGETMAN folder in the other.

Louisa and Ann watched as Beans put the folder on the work surface before opening her briefcase. She got out the vial of dark fingerprint powder.

Digging into her jeans pockets, she then took out a small reel of Sellotape.

'Are you going to dust the glasses for fingerprints?' asked Ann, surprised.

Beans nodded.

'What on earth for?' Louisa frowned.

'Did you notice the sergeant?' Beans asked, as she dusted fingerprint powder all round each glass.

'What about him?' Louisa asked.

'His jaw-line in particular,' Beans hinted.

She brushed the excess powder off the prints and straightened up with a smile. 'A perfect set of prints on both glasses.' Beans grinned.

'His skin was paler on the lower half of his face,' Louisa shrugged. 'So what?'

'Louisa, you haven't read the section in my dad's book on disguises.' Beans smiled with satisfaction. 'Because if you had, you'd know that when a bearded man shaves off his beard, especially in the summer, the skin beneath the beard is invariably going to be lighter than the rest of his face. It's the same for black men as well as white men.'

'So Sergeant Paxman had a beard until recently. So wha . . . ?' Louisa's voice trailed off as she realized what she'd said. 'You're not saying . . . he can't be . . . !' Louisa stared.

'You mean . . . Sergeant Paxman and Lucas Moynahan are one and the same person?' Ann breathed.

'That's exactly what I mean,' Beans replied.

'But they can't be. What would Lucas Moynahan be doing with Detective Warner?' Ann shook her head.

'Who told you he was Detective Warner? Who told you he was a detective? *He* did,' Beans said. Her tone was angry, but Louisa knew that Beans was angry with herself rather than anyone else. 'It's all my fault. Dad's always warning me not to let anyone into the house—the gas people, the electricity people, anyone—without scrutinizing their identification cards first. He waves his wallet under my nose and I just assumed it was all right.

I never had a proper, long look.'

As Beans spoke, she used the Sellotape to carefully lift the fingerprints off the glasses and place them on a clean piece of paper. She put the Sellotape back into her pocket and carried on talking.

'D'you know what I think happened? I reckon Lucas Moynahan shaved off his beard and wore sunglasses and extra layers of clothing to disguise himself. Did you see how squidgy and strange his shape was? I'll bet you anything that was padding underneath his outer clothes. He was trying to make sure that none of us would recognize him changing his hairstyle, padding himself out, shaving off his beard. Only he was a little too smart for his own good. Or he reckoned we were more stupid than we are!'

'But why?' Ann asked, bewildered. 'I mean, what did he hope to gain?'

'I think they were hoping to find me alone. Yesterday, so-called Detective Warner questioned me very closely about when Gran would be in, but I reckon now that he was more interested in when Gran would be *out.* They wanted to get me as well, to force Dad to tell them how the induction oscillator works. And if they couldn't get me, then Dad's notes or blueprints on the oscillator would be the next best thing. That Lucas Moynahan had to disguise himself or I would never have let him in. And he couldn't risk being seen by our neighbours, in case I had told someone about him and they gave his real description to the police.'

'Detective Warner didn't need to disguise himself because he was already in disguise. You already thought he was a detective,' Louisa gasped. 'So those two are the kidnappers . . . What a pair of cow pats! We have to go to the police. Right this second . . .'

'Oh no!' Beans straightened up suddenly, her expression stricken, horrified.

'What's the matter?' Ann asked. 'What is it?'

'Dad's letter—the one with the secret message,' Beans said, dismayed. 'I gave it to so-called Detective Warner.

They knew right from the start what Dad did. Oh, how could I have been so stupid? I got Dad into even more trouble.'

'You weren't to know,' Ann said. 'None of us were.'

'But what about the letter? How can I go to the police? That letter was proof that Dad's been kidnapped,' Beans whispered. 'I haven't got anything else.'

'What about the fingerprints the kidnappers left on the glasses?' Louisa asked.

Her lips a hard, anxious line, Beans took out her magnifying glass and started closely examining the fingerprints she'd just got off the glasses, comparing them to the fingerprints she'd recorded on Friday evening.

Ann crossed her fingers so tightly that they started to hurt. She and Louisa both peered over Beans's shoulder.

'I knew it!' Beans squealed.

'What is it?' Ann asked, moving in for a better look.

'Remember I took some fingerprints off the door handle of Dad's workroom?' Beans said. 'Look at that! This one matches up exactly with the right-hand little-finger print of Lucas Moynahan, taken from the prints I just got off his glass.'

'Are you sure?' Louisa asked.

'Look for yourself. It's got a whorl pattern with a ridge count of three,' Beans said.

'It's got a *what*?' Louisa blinked.

'Read Dad's book as I keep telling you! It's all explained in there,' Beans said. 'You know what this means, don't you? To my knowledge, Lucas Moynahan has never been in Dad's workroom, and I bet he'd deny even being in this house. Why should he have been in here? Dad doesn't know him. Their only connection is Dad's building society. So what were his fingerprints doing on Dad's workroom door handle? Lucas was here, both as Sergeant Paxman and as Lucas Moynahan. These fingerprints will prove it's one and the same man.'

'What about the one who calls

162

himself Detective Warner?' Louisa asked. 'Who's he, then?'

'The accomplice of that creep, Lucas Moynahan. He's no more a detective than I am,' Ann said with disgust.

'You girls are too smart for your own good. We'll take that folder! And those fingerprints' The voice cracked out like a whiplash from behind them.

Bean's head spun round in dismay. Ann gasped. Louisa couldn't breathe. There, standing by the open kitchen window and listening to every word, was 'Detective' Julian Warner—one of the kidnappers!

Chapter Twelve

Animal Crunchies to the Rescue!

'RUN!' Beans shouted.

Ann and Louisa didn't need to be told twice! Beans snatched up her OPERATION GADGETMAN folder from the kitchen work surface, her piece of paper with all the fingerprints on it, and legged it after her friends.

'STOP! YOU GIRLS, STAY RIGHT THERE!' Julian Warner yelled after them.

164

Beans heard him rattle the kitchen door, then curse. She offered up a silent prayer. Thank goodness Gran had locked the kitchen door. What a shame she didn't do the same to the side gate! Beans wondered how much the so-called detective had heard. Enough—of that there was no doubt. Beans rammed her new evidence into the OPERATION GADGETMAN folder.

'Quick! The front door!' Louisa shouted.

Ann got to the door first. She tried to turn the latch. It slipped through her sweaty fingers before it opened. And there stood Lucas Moynahan.

'Ann . . .' Louisa urged desperately. Ann tried to push the door shut. Lucas stuck his foot in it and pushed.

'Help me! Quick!' Ann squealed. She pushed back against the door with all her might. Lucas's hand appeared round the door as he sought a grip. Beans launched herself against the door to help Ann. Lucas cursed fluently as he tried to push back.

'Louisa, quick! Do something!'

165

Beans hissed frantically.

Louisa slammed her fist against Lucas's fingers whilst stomping down on his foot. His hand and foot withdrew immediately, to be replaced by a whole string of words that Beans's gran wouldn't have approved of. The girls slammed the door.

CRASH! CRUNCH!

The sound of glass being shattered came from the kitchen.

'Upstairs! Now!' Louisa pulled at Beans. Beans pulled Ann after her.

'Detective Warner's coming through the kitchen window.' Ann's voice shook.

'That's why we're running, Ann!' Louisa puffed. 'Come on!'

On the landing they stopped, looking around desperately for somewhere to hide.

'Separate!' Beans whispered urgently.

The three girls spread out like ripples in a pond. Beans dived into her bedroom, slamming the door behind her. For the first time ever, she wished she had a lock on her door. Clutching the OPERATION GADGETMAN folder to her chest, Beans turned her head quickly from left to right. Where could she put the folder so that the kidnappers wouldn't find it? She ran over to the window. Should she throw it out? That was no good. They'd find it on the lawn.

Think. *Think.*

Sellotape . . . where was her Sellotape? In her pocket. Thank God! Beans ran over to her bed. She dropped the folder on to the duvet and pulled the Sellotape out of her pocket.

The kidnappers were in the hall. They were at the bottom of the stairs.

'JUST WAIT TILL WE CATCH YOU LOT . . .' Lucas yelled out.

Beans tore off a piece of tape and another and another, flinging each piece on the bed. One piece got slightly tangled but she didn't have time to straighten it out. With one hand, Beans held the folder in place whilst the other hand was used to tape it. Still holding on to the folder, she used the second and the third strips of Sellotape to secure it.

The pounding footsteps were getting closer.

The folder hung precariously. It looked too heavy for the Sellotape. Beans tore off another strip.

Footsteps on the landing.

Beans dived towards the window. She didn't have time to use the fourth piece of tape and she didn't want the kidnappers to know where she'd hidden the folder.

Don't drop. Oh please, don't drop! she thought, her whole body quaking violently. She'd taped the folder behind her headboard, but now she wished she hadn't. It wouldn't stay up. It *couldn't* stay up.

Beans fiddled with the window catch. It wouldn't open. Her fingers were all thumbs and it wouldn't open.

'Oh please . . .' Beans begged it.

The bedroom door burst open. Beans opened her mouth as wide as she could.

'HELP!' she screamed at the top of her voice.

'Scream one more time and you'll never see your father again!' Lucas

Moynahan stood in the doorway, his expression thunderous.

Beans's scream died in her throat.

'Where's my dad?' she whispered.

'That's better. That's much better. JULIAN, I'VE GOT HIS DAUGHTER!' Lucas called out to his friend. 'And I'll take that little folder of yours that's got our fingerprints in it.'

'What do you hope to gain? You can't kidnap all of us,' Beans said furiously.

'We don't intend to,' Lucas said silkily. 'You're the only one we need. We'll lock up the others. When your dad realizes we've got you, he'll see sense and tell us what we want to know.'

Every drop of blood in Beans's body turned icy. Fear gnawed at her stomach.

Think, Beans, *think*, she told herself.

She had to stay calm. She had to find a way of outwitting these crooks. Think.

'The police know about my dad being kidnapped. You can't hope to get away with this,' Beans said.

169

'The police don't know anything about your dad or you or the induction oscillator. You gave your letter to "Detective Warner"—remember? And by the time they do find out the truth, it'll be too late.' Lucas's broadening grin was horrible to watch.

'*Think* . . .'

'M-my dad's original letter to the building society. That explains all about the induction oscillator. As soon as the police . . .' The words froze and died on Beans's lips. 'You have that letter, don't you? I bet it went straight into your pocket as well as the five thousand odd pounds.'

Lucas grinned. 'And that five thousand is just the beginning. We're going to make millions. Like Julian said, you're smart. You take after your dad,' His grin faded abruptly. 'But there's such a thing as being too smart.'

'So the building society don't know about any of this?' Beans whispered.

Lucas Moynahan snorted. 'If your dad had got as far as typing in his card number, then it would've been different. But as it is . . .' He laughed.

170

'You should see them, the manageress and the security staff, running around like headless chickens trying to work out how that money disappeared. As far as they're concerned, the motor just started up at a certain time and all the money came out and dropped to the pavement.'

Beans remembered now. She hadn't even got as far as putting Dad's card in the slot. She was checking the card to make sure Dad really had brought out the right one and not one which had expired.

'With your dad's invention, we intend to bring bewilderment to a lot more banks and building societies up and down the country.'

'But Dad . . .'

Whatever Beans had been about to say was broken off by a yell from Ann, followed by, 'You let me go! Right this *second*!'

'Ann . . .' Beans took a step forward. Lucas took a step towards her, blocking her way.

'Listen,' Beans said quickly. 'You don't want me or my dad. You just want to know how the induction oscillator works.'

'But your dad's being very stubborn,' Lucas said, frost creeping into his voice. 'He won't tell us how it works. So you're, going to persuade him for us.'

'B-but I told you. Dad's notes on that gadget are either in his bedroom or in the attic. It would take you less than ten minutes to find them. Then you wouldn't need me or my dad. You wouldn't have to bother with us. We'd only slow you down,' Beans tried to stop her words from spilling out, faster and faster. She had to stay calm. She had to be convincing.

'I'm listening,' Lucas prompted.

'Dad's papers explain all about how the oscillator works. You could take the papers and the oscillator and be out of Cleevesdon in about fifteen minutes flat. Then there'd be no-one to stop you from robbing as many cash-dispenser machines as you like. And by the time Dad built another one and showed the police how it worked, you would be millionaires. *Zillionaires*!'

'Hhmm!' Lucas rubbed his now cleanly shaven chin.

A shriek echoed across the landing.

'You just wait, you bullying ape!' Louisa's voice was indignant—furious as well as frightened. 'You just wait till I tell my dad! Let go of me!'

Julian Warner appeared, Louisa and Ann held under either arm.

'Lucas, for goodness sake,' said Julian. 'What am I supposed to do with these two?'

'The papers are here, honest they are. I'm not lying,' Beans repeated urgently. 'Y—you could lock us all in Dad's workroom whilst you search, if you don't believe me. I lied about Gran taking the key with her, she didn't. So you can lock us in and we wouldn't be able to get out, even if we tried. If you padlock the door, and the hole in the roof is too high for any of us to reach, even if we were to stand on Dad's worktable. If you don't find Dad's papers within five minutes then you can take me with you to persuade Dad to change his mind.'

'We could just take you back with us

now and have done with it,' Julian said harshly.

Beans glared at him. How could she ever have thought he was a detective? In future, no-one was setting foot over her doormat unless they handed over a proper identification card first.

'No, Julian, I've had enough of all this dancing about. We've already had to move her father to your house. I want to get out of Cleevesdon with the oscillator and start getting some real money,' Lucas said. 'That was the deal.'

'But what about these three?' Julian asked.

'We've already got the oscillator in my car, so we just find the instructions and blow! I don't give a monkey's about these three. We can lock them up.'

'What about her dad?' Julian nodded in Beans's direction.

'He'll be safe enough in your cellar. By the time anyone finds him, we'll be long gone,' said Lucas.

'I don't know . . . I don't like it . . .' Julian said slowly.

'Listen! The longer we hang about here, the more likely we are to get caught. I want to get out of this dump of a town as soon as possible,' said Lucas angrily. 'Better ten minutes here than a forty-minute drive back to your house and more time wasted, persuading her dad that he should talk to us.'

'Will you put me down?' Louisa fumed.

Ann and Louisa were still struggling to get free. Beans hardly dared breathe. She wanted her and her friends to get away from the kidnappers. She *needed* to be locked up in Dad's workroom.

'These instructions . . .' Lucas turned to Beans, his eyes narrowed suspiciously. 'Will we understand them?'

'Oh, of course you will. Dad always writes out his notes so any idio . . . so anyone can understand. If I'd seen his notes I would tell you how the oscillator works myself. I just want you two to go away,' Beans said. 'And like I said, if you don't find them, you can always come back for me.'

'Well, if we don't find them, or if we find the instructions and you need to be a rocket scientist to understand them, I'll be very annoyed at you for wasting our time,' said Lucas softly. 'Do you understand me? *Very annoyed.*'

'I understand.' Beans swallowed hard.

Lucas marched over to her and grabbed her by the wrist. 'You'd better tell your friends to behave themselves. I don't want any nosy neighbours calling the police because they see you lot struggling.'

'Ann, Louisa, please,' Beans pleaded.

Julian put her friends on to their feet and stepped back to block the doorway. Ann and Louisa scowled at both men, but especially Julian. Beans blinked rapidly at them. She had to make them understand. They had to play-along with her dad's kidnappers— at least for now.

The two men followed Beans, Ann and Louisa out of the house. Beans's heart was ready to explode out of her body. Her mouth was dry, her palms sticky. In the garden, she turned to Julian.

'W—Why didn't you just search the house for Dad's notes or the oscillator blueprints when you were pretending to be a detective?' she asked. All the while, Beans's glance kept creeping back to her neighbour's house.

Lucas answered before his accomplice could. 'Because we never really wanted that stuff. We were after you from the beginning,' he sneered. 'Only you were never alone, so we couldn't grab you.

'And I couldn't risk searching over your house again in case you or your gran got suspicious and maybe asked to see my ID properly,' said Julian icily. 'But now we have no choice. You three know who we really are, so we're going to take your dad's notes and disappear.'

'So we'd better find them—and fast,' Lucas said directly to Beans. 'If you're playing games . . .' He didn't need to say any more.

Beans dug her fingernails into her palms and forced herself to walk at the same pace. She couldn't let them know that she was up to something. How long would she have before they came back to the workroom to get her? Would she have enough time . . . ?

Less than a minute later, the three girls had been locked up in the workroom—after Julian had checked that they indeed couldn't reach the roof of the workroom if they stood on the table.

When Beans heard the key turn in the padlock outside, for the first time in what seemed like hours she allowed herself to relax. She sighed with relief and leaned back against the sturdy wooden door.

'Quick, you two,' she hissed. 'We don't have much time. They'll be back soon.'

'You have a plan?' said Ann, eagerly.

'Of course I've got a plan. You don't think I'm going to let them get away with it, do you?' Beans said scornfully. 'But I needed them to put us in Dad's workroom first.'

'We're here. Now what?' asked Louisa.

'We need to get that tarpaulin down.

Ann, you stand on Dad's table and I'll pass the broom up to you.Thank God my gran can't see one square centimetre of space without tidying it! Otherwise we'd never find everything we need before those two dworps came back,' Beans said. 'Louisa, you get out some elastic bands from the end drawer. The thick, long, strong ones. And line up those animal crunchies Dad was experimenting with on the table.'

'Right!' Louisa grinned.

It took several agonizing, anxious moments before Ann finally shifted the tarpaulin aside. She jumped down off the table.

'I've done my bit,' said Louisa. 'What next?'

'Hang loads of long bits of Sellotape from the doorframe to get in their faces. And we need something to trip them up when they come in here,' Beans said. 'Let's get out the light bulbs and line those up as well. They'll be perfect for chucking.'

One of Dad's current projects was making an everlasting light bulb. He hadn't succeeded yet—but he had enough light bulbs in his workroom to keep the whole house permanently lit for at least the next ten years.

They all got busy, getting any and everything out of the drawers and boxes that could be used as weapons.

'The most important thing is to make a lot of noise,' said Beans, glancing down apprehensively at her watch. 'Are the animal crunchies lined up? Louisa, you and me are going to put an elastic band between our fingers and use it like a catapult.'

'I get you. We send the animal crunchies flying!' Louisa said.

'Exactly. And Ann, you can stand at the side there and get them with the broom handle the moment they walk through the door. Then you get back here and start hurling the light bulbs and whatnot at them.'

'I get all the good jobs.' Ann grinned, picking up the broom.

'Louisa, try to catapult some of the animal crunchies out the open hole in the roof as well,' Beans said.

'Why? Surely . . .' Louisa began.

'Shush! I think they're coming back,' Ann hissed.

Immediately they all fell silent. The crunch of heavy footsteps on the dry garden grass could be heard. Ann took up position by the door. Louisa and Beans armed their makeshift catapults. Beans didn't dare breathe in case she gave the game away.

This was it . . .

The key turned in the padlock. The door opened.

'Right then, Beatrice Conran. I warned you . . .'

'GO!' Beans shouted.

TWANG!

The elastic in each girl's catapult leapt forward. The animal crunchie whizzed towards the two men. One flew over their heads before exploding. The other smacked Lucas in the chest before the blast went off. BOOOOM! BOOOOOOOM!

'What the . . .' Julian exclaimed, ducking.

Ann seized her chance, whilst Lucas was fighting off the strips of Sellotape and Julian was ducking out of the way of another exploding animal crunchie.

'Take that!' Ann shouted.

She whacked Lucas across the stomach with the broom handle.

'And that!' she screamed, swinging lower to whack Julian across his shins.

'Get them!' Louisa shouted, arming her catapult again.

'Ann, get back!' Beans yelled above the explosions going off all around them.

Ann carried on hitting out with her broom handle. Lucas made an angry grab for her. With a squeak, Ann leapt backwards out of his grasp, before running back to her friends.

'Wow! What a racket!' Ann whooped over the sound of another explosion.

'That's the idea!' Beans yelled back. 'If this doesn't get Mr McKee running to his phone to call the police, then I don't know what will.'

Your neighbour?' Ann shouted, puzzled. 'Of course. His threat on Friday morning.'

'You've got it!' Beans grinned. 'Reload with more than one crunchie at a time! GO!'

The noise was phenomenal. Like the sound of a whole volley of cannons going off at once.

BOOOOOOOOMMMMM!

Four or five animal crunchies went off simultaneously.

'My dad might have some weird ideas about making shortcake biscuits, but he knows his explosions!' Beans yelled proudly.

'You girls just wait!' Lucas shouted, ducking to avoid a volley of animal crunchies heading straight for him.

'Gotcha!' Ann leapt up and down as a well-targeted light bulb hit Julian square on the forehead.

Again and again, Beans and her friends loaded up with animal crunchies and light bulbs and anything else that would make a good weapon and sent them flying. Lucas and Julian couldn't get anywhere near the girls.

'Lucas, leave them. We'd better disappear before . . .'

But it was too late. Up the side path came Mr McKee.

'What's going on here?' Mr McKee ranted. 'I'll have all of you know that

I've called the police. I warned you . . .'

'MR MCKEE, HELP US! STOP THEM! THEY'VE KIDNAPPED MY DAD!' Beans screamed over and over.

Lucas and Julian made a break for it, but the attempt was hopeless. Mr McKee only needed a quick glance at Beans's frantic expression to know that something was going on. Lucas tried to barge past him. Mr McKee stuck out his foot and tripped him up, then he fell heavily on top of Lucas like some kind of all-in wrestler. Ann and Louisa went charging after Julian. Louisa jumped on his back, whilst Ann renewed her attack on his shins with the broom-stick handle. Julian sank to his knees in agony. Beans rushed over to Mr McKee, ready to help him with Lucas. Mr McKee didn't need much help! He was sitting on Lucas and had the man's arms twisted behind his back.

Mr McKee turned his head, a deep frown on his face. 'Beatrice, would you mind telling me what on earth is going on?'

*　　　*　　　*

Fifteen minutes later, Louisa, Ann and Beans were seated in the kitchen, explaining to Sergeant Spicer exactly what had happened.

'I was banking on Mr McKee calling the police,' Beans said. 'I didn't want Lucas and Julian to get away.'

'Don't worry. They're on their way to the police station,' smiled Sergeant Spicer. 'They won't be going anywhere in a hurry.'

Beans wanted to go with the police when they went to Julian Warner's house to pick up her dad, but Sergeant Spicer wouldn't allow it.

'It's best you wait here,' he said. 'I would've thought that you three girls could stand the rest!'

Beans spent the time watching the clock on the sitting-room wall. Each second seemed to take at least an hour to tick by.

'All this waiting is driving me crazy,' Beans admitted to Louisa and Ann. 'What if Dad . . .'

'No "what ifs"' Louisa said firmly.

185

'Your dad is on his way home right now And he's fine.'

'Yeah, of course he is,' Ann agreed. 'I just know he is.'

And she was right. An hour and ten minutes later, the front door opened.

'Beans! Beans, are you in there?'

'DAD!' Beans bounded off the sofa before anyone could stop her. She ran into the hall and flung herself at her father. He looked bone tired but very, very happy.

'Oh Dad, I was so worried,' Beans sniffed.

'It's over,' her dad smiled. 'I'm home now. And, the police tell me that it's all thanks to you.'

'And Louisa and Ann. I couldn't have done it without them,' Beans said, grinning at her friends who'd followed her into the hall.

'Thank you, Louisa,' Dad said to Louisa. He turned to Ann. 'And thank you, Ann. I won't forget it.'

'You're dead welcome, Mr C.,' Ann grinned, sniffing so her eyes wouldn't leak.

'Yeah. Dead welcome!' Louisa could

hardly get the words out.

The front door opened.

'What's going on? Why are all those people outside? Beans, I hope . . .' Gran froze as she saw her son. 'Daniel. You . . . you . . .' Gran covered the distance between them in about one second flat! She hugged Beans's father so tight that he started coughing. 'Daniel, I ought to clunk you over the head with my handbag! Are you all right? I was worried sick.'

'I'm fine, Mum,' Beans's dad smiled. 'I'm home now.'

'I hope this means that there'll be no more inventing,' Gran said sternly.

'You must be joking!' Beans's dad scoffed. 'In fact, being locked up gave me a chance to mull over a couple of new ideas I had for some really useful gadgets.'

'I was afraid of that,' Gran sighed. She pulled away, then smiled. 'I'm going to put the kettle on. I'm sure we could all do with a cup of tea. Oh yes, and don't hit the roof but I tidied your workroom. The place was a mess.'

'I'm not going to hit the roof, Mum,'

Beans's dad smiled. 'I'm too glad to be home.'

'If anything, you should thank me for my efforts,' Gran retorted, heading towards the kitchen. 'In all my days I've never seen anything in such a state. The house was a mess. Your workroom was worse . . .' She walked into the kitchen, still muttering under her breath.

Beans and her dad looked at each other.

'Nag! Nag! Nag!' they whispered in unison.

Gran's head appeared from around the kitchen door.

'I heard that!' she smiled.